D1251347

Rachel

Rachel

IVAN SOUTHALL

Farrar Straus Giroux
NEW YORK

Also by Ivan Southall

Hills End
Ash Road
The Fox Hole
To the Wild Sky
Sly Old Wardrobe
Let the Balloon Go
Finn's Folly
Chinaman's Reef Is Ours
Walk a Mile and Get Nowhere
   (Bread and Honey)
Josh
Benson Boy
   (Over the Top)
Head in the Clouds
Matt and Jo
What About Tomorrow?
King of the Sticks
The Golden Goose
The Long Night Watch

Contents

Contents

CHAPTER ONE

Law-abiding People

When Rachel grew up in Donkey Gully most law-abiding people had a shotgun over the fireplace.

It was a nice dry spot for it. Conspicuous, too, if furtively sighted from outside, a declaration to the roughs and the toughs, "Clear off".

Some said the shotgun was a carry-over from earlier days; an insurance against their return. There was always a restlessness in the air. Even a glorious day was in some way imperfect — if you were sensitive to the subtleties of atmosphere.

Dad had been a kid in the old days when the rich made thousands and thousands and the poor made a bit from time to time, though usually blew it before a week was through and at once were poor again.

Well, being poor was a state of mind, Dad said, same as being rich. And he was the one to know. If things changed too drastically, he said, you got scared.

Rachel had been nothing then, in the old days. The same went for Rennie and Rose, only more so. Before Being Born. The whole wide world in chaos, but no Rachel, or Rennie or Rose, to add their share.

"Life's full of these odd little facts," Dad said.

Dad hung the gun up over where the mantelpiece would be, not long after Rachel turned two, when the house was new, as soon as he'd built the chimney and put the doors on and the windows in and the floorboards in place and could lock the thieves out. No good hanging up the gun if some light-fingered rogue was going to reach it down.

"A gun's a beautiful mechanism for the work it has to do," Dad said. "Man's work. Looking after you."

Rachel never came to dispute the point and only one other person ever reached the gun down, Auntie Lizzie, on Election Eve, 14 July, the Friday Willie the Ferret laboriously wrote *I am a rat* on the blackboard forty-seven times, signing each line William Hobson Herbert. Not that being both ferret and rat stretched Willie's talents very far.

Auntie Lizzie moved in when Rachel was five — eight years before Election Eve. She was Dad's big sister. Well, she'd been bigger for a while when he was little, as Auntie Susie had been, too. That was long ago.

Rachel pointed to the gun. "That's man's work, Auntie Lizzie. Do you know how to fire it if Dad's not here when the bad men come?"

"I was shooting rabbits through the left eyebrow before your father could recite his two-times table," Auntie Lizzie said, closing her right eye and inclining her head as if squinting along the sights.

That was good news.

"How many bad men have you shot through the left eyebrow, Auntie Lizzie?"

"Awful lot of one-eyebrowed bad men round here. Hadn't you noticed? Hardly a bad man with two eyebrows to keep the rain out."

On wild winter nights down the years, when the door was locked and the fire burned bright and the yellow lamps flickered and the gun gleamed and Dad wasn't there, Rachel knew she was safe with Auntie Lizzie. Well, until she grew a little older and a little wiser.

Not that Donkey Gully ripped and roared as it used to, thank goodness. Desperadoes weren't leaning against verandah posts any more, and hold-ups didn't happen often, and no one had hung from a local tree in years, except the few who tied the knot themselves. But the roughnecks were there. Young and old.

They lived in caves and abandoned mine-workings in

the Devil's Hot Pot, Nature's great ditch, sometimes showing their faces in town, but never taking much away unless they brought in gold to trade. Later they'd be reeling and tumbling and staggering home to wherever or whatever home might be, or sleeping it off under a tree, the rain pouring down.

Rachel tried not to see them, tried not to think about it, for it perplexed her.

Dad called them the debris of gone-away years, and said, "Something good may be locked away inside, but assume otherwise. I regret having to say this. The younger they are, the more dangerous they are."

Sometimes after church Dad took the gun and went shooting rabbits and hares — for what the adults in the house amusingly called "a welcome change of diet" — along with almost everybody else old enough to pull a trigger. Mobs even walked across country from the townships higher up. Going off to church was what the grown-ups liked to call a calculated risk.

Hunting dogs were barking and shots were reverberating through the gullies from first light onwards. Talk about the day of rest. You got more rest at school in the middle of the week when Carter Hooke wasn't looking.

Poor rabbits. Poor hares.

A reckless creature it was who poked its nose out of its burrow of a Sunday.

There was the time the preacher raised his arm to start performing about God's terrifying threats to wicked children (who were uncommonly numerous round about). He knew how to put the case, with flashing eyes and fiery cheeks and hair flopping up and down. But the day was Rachel's.

Barry Basset, the barber's son, down from the high road with his father's gun, at that moment blasted a rabbit to Kingdom Come a mere fifteen paces from the church front door.

The effect was shocking.

Shocking what the church stewards did to Master

Basset. The barber said none of them should come back to him for a shave if they were interested in a nice clean job.

The barber, not known as a god-fearing man, was not distressed to hear that several ladies of the congregation apparently fainted.

"If they can't stand the sound of an honest gun," he said, "they should take a ship back to where they came from."

But Dizzy Hobson, of the Pig Creek Hobsons, screamed for a minute and a half and had to be silenced with a peppermint, firmly administered, and Miss Petersen seated at the organ went off completely in what proved to be a distressing scene, not forgotten by anyone who witnessed it, not even eighty years afterwards.

Kids whispered behind their hands, "She's gone off her bean again."

The following Sunday a new organist took Miss Petersen's place, as new as any organist of whom anyone round about had reliable report. She was nine at the time. Rachel.

"As sad as it has to be," Dad said, "one man's poison can be another man's meat."

Rachel sat at the organ, in a haze, in a daze, in a glow.

Rose said, "That's my sister."

Rennie said, "That's my sister."

Auntie Lizzie said, "That's my niece."

Dad said, "That's Bell's daughter and she's not alive to feel the pride."

From time to time Rachel went on these shooting expeditions with Dad, hunting rabbits and hares for the welcome change of diet, nervously tiptoeing behind, expecting to be shot from some unguarded direction, shutting her eyes and gritting her teeth whenever Dad raised the gun. All of it being such an agony she wondered why she went at all. Perhaps to hold Dad's hand on the way home. A girl had to have a bit of her dad for her very own.

Rabbit pie was fair enough if there wasn't anything else, but hare was awful. It used to be left hanging round the house in a wire safe going rotten.

"You can't enjoy hare unless it's mature," Auntie Lizzie said. "Waste of good hare if it's not ripe. Like a green apple."

Rachel had a text hanging over her fireplace on top of the gun.

Terrible place for it to be.

Years ago Mother worked the text on linen, with flowers and scrolls and birds. Dad set it in an elaborate frame that took him, in his leisure time, about three weeks with a fretsaw.

> *The Lord is the Head of this House,*
> *the Unseen Guest at Every Meal.*

Something that might have been called the absolute statement.

Rachel said, "I bet He doesn't come when we have hare. I bet he says *urrgh* and goes to Mrs Hobson next door. She's civilised. She's a vegetarian."

Auntie Lizzie frowned on that. Oh dear, yes. Closed one eye (as if shooting out a bad man's left eyebrow), pursed her lips, *frowned*.

"I'm sorry," Rachel said, looking at the floor.

"As well you ought, my girl. Jugged hare is one of the Lord's special delicacies."

Though she knew that Auntie Lizzie felt very strongly about this (and no one in the world, except Dad, was more important than Auntie Lizzie), Rachel felt sure that the Lord preferred savoury mince the way vegetarians made it, because blood was not spilt and no beautiful living creature suffered or missed a moment of the wonderful world.

"What page is the recipe for jugged hare on, Auntie Lizzie?" Rachel said.

"How do you expect me to remember a thing like that?"

"I think you ought to, if it's so very important."

Auntie Lizzie began to look wary. "The chapter on game," she said. "Where else?"

"I don't remember seeing that in the Bible, Auntie Lizzie."

"You don't find recipes in the Bible! You get them out of Mrs Beeton."

"Did God write Mrs Beeton, too, Auntie Lizzie?"

Auntie Lizzie made a buzzing sound, not uncommon during these searching conversations. And glanced across the paddocks towards Mrs Hobson next door, Mrs Myrtle Hobson, formerly Myrtle Herbert, of the back road Herberts, the religious cranks. A very searching glance it was too.

"Rachel," said Auntie Lizzie, "run along. Learn your spelling for tomorrow."

"It's learnt, Auntie Lizzie."

"Well, let me hear your music practice."

"You must've heard it, Auntie Lizzie. It's done."

Auntie Lizzie went on making buzzing sounds. "Child, take a basket, get moving, gather me some mushrooms."

"Mushrooms don't grow at this time of year, Auntie Lizzie."

"If I say gather mushrooms, you gather them, whether they grow or not."

Rachel took the basket. She was smart enough to be top of the class when the clever ones were sick.

It was disturbing when you thought about it, though, the text and the shotgun one above the other, the declaration from God and the threat from man in full view. If you saw one, you had to see the other.

Take note! Be warned! You're under scrutiny!

Man's reaction to bad behaviour could be predicted without difficulty. God's reaction raised questions, because there was that fellow every Sunday jumping up and down in the pulpit.

Perhaps God'd say to the devil, "I don't want Rachel. You can have her for a kitchen maid."

Glory be. Stirring cauldrons of boiling oil for evermore just because you were feeling a bit high-spirited or had spent a couple of hours behind a tree with a book.

Did they expect you to devote your *whole* life to entertaining little sisters? Did they want you growing up ignorant, having to sign your name with an X, never having heard of the Reverend E. P. Roe, for instance, or *Miss Lou?*

"Miss who?" Dad said. "And this reverend fellow. Who's he? Don't tell me there's one I don't know."

"You're real ignorant," Rachel said. "And do you know why? Because you didn't read books when you were a boy. Because you spent your time running round screaming and shouting. Auntie Lizzie told me."

In time Rachel came to learn that remarks of this kind led to wisdom.

At home, Dad was the judge of behaviour, based on Auntie Lizzie's reports of it, God being known to take Dad's word for it, the same as Dad took Auntie Lizzie's word for it. No one under the age of twenty-one stood a chance.

At school, Carter Hooke was judge, jury, and executioner.

Hooke, the headmaster, the long, bony, rangy fellow with the sallow skin and the pince-nez bifocals, the left lens of which having long since half broken off. Hooke, the widower with the tired eyes and the tired stoop and the heavy sigh and the nightly prayer (so it was said), "Father in Heaven, Prince of Patience, Fountain of Mercy, deliver me from this place."

At home time on 9 June, about five weeks before Election Eve, when half the kids had left the classroom, Hooke called, "Rachel, you'll wait."

Oh, my goodness gracious, thought Rachel, and turned pale. I haven't done a single thing I shouldn't have done. I just know. Someone's been telling lies about me. My birthday Sunday and all. And Rennie and Rose will've heard and they'll run all the way home. "Rachel's kept in, Auntie Lizzie. Rachel's been bad. The family's in disgrace."

She sat back at her desk, her face going long, her spirits flowing down into the floor through her big toes.

The future was a huge dark cloud.

Carter Hooke shut the door.

"Rachel Lefevre, according to my records, you turn thirteen Sunday, making you a big girl. As I've often said, living round here's like living in a jungle and it'll be driving me to drink like every headmaster before me. I've been seeing you Tuesdays and Fridays walking the high street after school. It won't do. I know your music lessons are later than they used to be, but you tell Miss Herbert I say you're to wait indoors. Starting today. And afterwards hurry home. Never allow the thought to enter a single head that you're loitering and have nowhere to go. I wish you didn't live so far out of town. At this time of year, particularly, I wish your father didn't work so late down the mine."

CHAPTER TWO

Willie Herbert's Nose

Miss Herbert taught piano behind the family shop in the high road that went on to Ballarat, the fabulous city of gold, the capital of the world, where Heinze's sold the most marvellous pork sausages you were likely to see in or out of a shop window. The Herberts didn't sell sausages of any kind.

They were known as the high road Herberts, a necessary distinction because Herberts were numerous: the high road Herberts, the low road Herberts, the old road Herberts, the new road Herberts, the Herberts on the hill, the Herberts in the gully, and so on. The same went for Hobsons and Crawfords.

Actually, there were two Miss Herberts teaching piano. When Rachel went in for her twice-weekly lesson after school, Miss Nora might be there, or Miss Sarah. Hardly ever were they there together.

"Do you think they're witches," kids said, "and take turns to fly away? We ought to set a watch on the nights there's a moon. They look like witches; look just like Willie; ferret faces and all. I wonder where the high road Herberts got their faces from? When faces were being dished out, they must've got in the animal queue."

Others reckoned Miss Nora and Miss Sarah had a husband in Ballarat, but the poor fellow couldn't stand the sight of more than one of them at a time.

"They're not witches," Willie wailed. "My aunties wouldn't have a husband without telling me. They go to look after Great Uncle Horrie in Sebastopol. And they're real good lookin', like me. There's a real good view of me side on. A real high intelligent forehead."

"That's because you're goin' bald," kids said.

When Rachel was still very young she favoured the sausage theory, because it would be impolite to ask the Misses Herbert to explain. If you lived in Ballarat you could have pork sausages every day. Perhaps the sisters came home week about to earn enough for a few more then dashed back again.

It was common talk that it was worth the trip to Ballarat just to get your foot in Heinze's door. High adventure in the train. Some who did the trip only once bragged about it for years. Others who did it every day had status. Real status. Like the kids who went on to Continuation School. The kids with money or brains. Lucky dogs. Hardly a Herbert face, or a Hobson, or a Crawford among them.

Going to Ballarat by road wasn't bad either. That sparkling white road of crushed quartz flashing in the sun like diamonds, probably full of little bits of gold. You didn't notice when you walked up and down to local school each day; you didn't realise how terribly important it was, until you found it going on and on, sparkling all the way to the city of gold.

The other direction was different. Donkey Gully!

Who'd want to go out there except to shoot a rabbit and leave again?

The Devil's Hot Pot was down there, too, the place to keep away from, unless you were stupid or a hero. Even away from the edges of it. They could catch you underfoot and carry you off. The tales some kids came back to relate behind the shelter sheds fair turned you cold.

Bad men lived down there in caves. Every kid knew that some had been chained up by the devil and that blood dripping from the walls of their prisons turned to red steam. At midnight, if you couldn't sleep, you might hear their awful cries, though it could have been the Tantanoola Tiger that had been lurking about the

fringes of one township or another for years, tearing
sheep to pieces and terrifying children, even giving the
grown-ups a few scares.

An awful place, that old Devil's Hot Pot. Cruel cliffs,
massive boulders about to topple and fall, and crashing
waters below. You didn't go there, if you were an
ordinary mortal, unless a grown-up held you by the hand.

Rachel went but once. Went with Dad, round the long
way, the safer way, where there weren't so many mine
shafts, a half-hour buggy ride round by the back road,
then a long walk in through the stony rises, tightly
holding hands.

Rennie held Rachel's hand and Rose held Rennie's
hand and Dad's most distant hand at the far end was in
possession of the gun.

When they came to look down into the gorge, Rachel
knew she had to say something, had to sound brave, had
to look brave, had to bluff those little sisters: "God's just
got to know where Captain Moonlight hid his ill-gotten
hoard in this old Devil's Hot Pot. All that gold. All that
silver. All those diamonds and watches and necklaces and
rings and brooches and gentlemen's tie-pins with tiger-
eyes. Why doesn't He show us where? Then we can buy a
new organ. That awful old thing. Always squeaking and
groaning and missing its notes. Just because I'm a kid
they think I don't notice. No wonder Miss Petersen went
off her bean."

Rennie, next to Rachel, was having one of her
practical days. "My teacher says Pig Creek took
thousands of years to cut this place out of the ground.
What's the devil got the credit for?"

Rose, who was nearly five at that particular time, said
at length, "After the devil cooks the bad people in his hot
pot. After he makes the pies out of them. After he puts
the crust all round. After that does he sell the pies in his
shop or will he eat them himself with tomato sauce on
them?"

While Rachel was trying to work this out, Rennie said, "Of course he doesn't put tomato sauce on them. He puts sugar on them to sweeten them up because they're made out of bad people. He'd put tomato sauce on them if he made them out of you."

"I'm not big enough to make a pie out of," Rose cried, "am I, Daddy?"

Rachel was sure she'd make a very large pie indeed, but Dad in answer to these various questions and comments thoughtfully said, "The world's full of mysteries, boys, as I've told you before."

An annoying habit, this, calling them boys. Who'd want to be one of those?

However, after that, he carried Rose for a while in his strong left arm, the right one having the gun in it, and whispered in her ear, loud enough for Rachel to hear, "Of course you're too small to make a pie out of. The devil doesn't like sweetie pies, anyway. He likes them big and fat. He likes them all bulbous and bulging. He likes them all horrible and bitter."

Strange tastes.

Next Dad carried Rennie, who was only seven then, and whispered firmly and distinctly in her ear because on some days Rennie was quite deaf, "That's a very good question, sweetheart, about the devil getting the credit for it. Some people are always getting the credit for things they don't deserve. Take Councillor Dave Hobson, for instance. And others get the blame and don't deserve that either. Look at your poor father."

Rachel didn't get to be carried. That was the worst of being church organist. Everyone expected you to be grown up. Even your dad. So little sisters got carried and had special things whispered in their ears. When you were ten you got nothing.

That night, though, when Dad tucked Rachel into bed, he *did* whisper in her ear.

"God can't use tainted money to put a better organ in the church. You know that. It's got to be clean money, earned by the sweat of our brows."

"What about my brow, then? Give a thought to the sweat on that. Pumping away at that old thing and having grunts and wheezes coming out of it."

So what did he say? Not a word, except a kind of clicking sound, meaning much the same as Auntie Lizzie's buzzing sound. Maybe they got born to be people by mistake. Maybe they were meant to be insects. Then Dad blew out the candle and left everything in the dark, except the tiny blue flame of the night-light on the shelf near the door, specially there to keep the spooks away from Rachel, and headed off down to the kitchen to play cribbage with Auntie Lizzie.

"Fifteen two, fifteen four, fifteen six, and a pair makes eight."

Grown-up arithmetic tables were different from the ones kids had to learn.

In the shop up on the high road, behind which the Misses Herbert taught piano, the brothers Sam, Dick, and Bob Herbert sold planks for lining walls and laying floors if the house you were building had need of them. Many of the houses round about (even some of those occupied by other Herberts) were made of materials closer to Nature. The high road Herberts also sold roofing iron, wallpaper, and toffee apples in season.

They were, in fact, very fond of toffee apples themselves, except when they started going sticky in sultry weather. Then they'd been known to give them away free, so the toffee wouldn't get on the wallpaper. First come, first served, one toffee apple per customer.

The news had been known to travel far, far out of sight in minutes. Some of the maiden ladies round about said it was an honest-to-goodness hometown demonstration of the powers of supernatural telepathic communication.

Rarely got as far as the gully, though, in time for the kids
out there to do anything about it. Much, much too far to
run. Time only to fret and fume.

In her long career as a kid at the gully, Rachel never
got a smell of a sticky toffee apple, despite her being behind that shop twice a week, seated at the piano, with one
Miss Herbert or the other rapping her knuckles with a
lead pencil. The local kids, lucky them, when the signal
went out, would be leaving their dinner tables with gravy
on their faces, or even tumbling off their lavatory seats
and rushing into view with their pants unbuttoned,
begging passers-by, please, to button them up, hurry,
hurry, because Sam, Dick and Bob had been known to
refuse toffee apples to kids whose pants were half off.
Well, why not? If Rachel had had her way, those toffee
apples would have been reserved for well-bred, well-
mannered, softly spoken young ladies.

Talk about a boys' world.

The battle paddock next door to Herberts' shop was
another department of the boys' world, then came the
odd-looking structure, once huge and now partly dis-
mantled, called Scatty School by the kids, even by Rachel,
who was so polite you could hardly believe it, and lived
in a law-abiding manner in a proper house. Of course the
kids who lived in mud huts never called it less than Scatty
and often called it more, along with the real wild kids
who lived with the pigs and the chooks and perhaps
bathed in the wash-up dish on Saturday nights if their
mothers could catch them, which was not often, if Carter
Hooke was to be believed. "It's a wonder," he said, "they
don't break down into humus."

Every schoolday these kids trooped in from far and
wide, even from Donkey Gully, presenting a reasonable
facade first thing Monday. Facade it was. By home time
of the same day Carter Hooke would be hurrying to get
outside for a breath of fresh air and a bit of grown-up

conversation, if the infant mistress hadn't already made her escape.

Friday saw Hooke's working week at breaking point. He'd had enough of children, of pupil teachers, of headaches, of backaches, of bellyaches, of wielding that long leather strap in the pursuit of lost causes, and notably of the accumulated effect of so many unwashed bodies six days on from last bath night.

Hardly any child was ever kept in, for obvious reasons, unless the crime committed was determined, insolent, frightful, and set dangerous precedents. Like the episode of Willie the Ferret and the going-home bell on Friday, 14 July, Election Eve; the bell being rung late, deliberately, provocatively, out of sheer witless defiance, by two minutes and twenty seconds, reducing Hooke's weekend of recuperation by the same margin, and further reducing it by the hour given to punishment, the length of time taken by Willie to cover the blackboard, from top to bottom and side to side, with the signed statement that he was a rat.

"If power corrupts kings who are born to power," Hooke said the following day to Mr Frank Lefevre Junior, Rachel's dad, "here we have a demonstration of what it does to wretched little boys. Look at the problems caused."

As for the battle paddock next door to Scatty School, horses might be seen grazing there. Coach horses. Splendid animals. Sometimes oats were growing there. Sometimes shrieking kids were there after school cheering on their favourites, Crawfords into Herberts, or Herberts into Hobsons, or one of the many variations on the theme. Hooke let them go. His limit was past by then. His philosophy was that pain or unconsciousness inflicted by boys upon each other out of school hours was to be regarded with gratitude and thanksgiving.

Sometimes the walking wounded limped bloodily into

the shop and the Miss Herbert who happened to be home
that week would be called to patch them up, particularly
if their families settled their accounts at the shop each
month with gold that Father might have puddled on the
less hazardous reaches of the infamous Pig Creek.

This was the course of events on Election Eve when
Willie, the bell monitor, recklessly abused his power, and
mobs of boys in opposition patrolled the high road
outside in full view of Willie at the blackboard.

It was Crawfords against Herberts mainly, with
Hobsons undecided. No violence in the early stages, but
plenty of abuse, and much manoeuvring for position,
Willie's indiscretion being the best legitimate excuse for
a pitched battle in months. Friday night was perfect. The
whole weekend for thick lips and black eyes and squashed
noses to return to good condition.

Three girls only were to be seen. The Herbert sisters
from Gipsy Valley Road. The wild ones. The tomboys.
Always a terrible problem, even for a hoodlum. You
couldn't hit them even if they were coming at you with a
log of wood. The only honourable thing to do was run.

They were a complication, a real complication, while
the Crawfords were trying to position themselves to cover
the exits from the school and the fences at the same time.
Then there was the need to get the Hobsons on side,
or at least neutral and not on the other side. But these
girls, these wild girls! Willie really had friends in the right
places. First cousins. Kissing cousins maybe. Who needed
Continuation School if you had cousins like these?

Eddie Crawford was the general. The Herberts were a
rabble. With Eddie in the job, did any other side stand a
chance, even with the Herbert sisters counted in?

Shopkeepers were getting nervous, particularly Sam,
Dick and Bob Herbert whose windows were nearest. The
news had long since reached Sam, twenty times at least,
that Willie was late home for reasons well known from
one end of the town to the other. And what could you do

about it? No good taking Hooke to task. In his position wouldn't you have done the same — or worse? And was Hooke responsible for the Herberts, the Hobsons and the Crawfords? He didn't come onto the scene until that situation was as nicely settled as day and night.

Hooke, like everybody else, was its victim.

And could Sam walk along to the school, to the gate, and wait, to escort his son home?

Impossible. It was a long-established principle going back a couple of generations. Willie would never be able to hold up his head again if Sam did that.

And were there enough willing men round about to order this mob of kids home as representing a threat to the public good? Not enough in sight anyway.

Able-bodied or public-spirited men were working out on the farms or down the mines or, because it was Friday, were already drunk at the pub. No one could reasonably be asked to send fourscore young hoodlums packing, except the policeman. If you could find him. Were you ever able to find him if the kids were running wild? He'd spent the day in court in Ballarat, and naturally the mail coach bringing him back home was as late as it had been in a month. An axle or a wheel or a shaft? Not a sight or a sound. Not even a distant volley of shots that could have signalled an interesting turn of events on the road. Nothing sounding like a gun except the slam of the school main door as Hooke threw Willie out, Willie yelling, "No, Mr Hooke, I don't want to go home tonight."

But Willie was out and the front door was shut and Carter Hooke was slipping out the back door and walking briskly across the deserted schoolyard to the headmaster's cottage, where he intended to reduce the level in the bottle of his best dry sherry by a thumb's length at least.

Thus Willie and various groups of Herberts, Crawfords and Hobsons were fully engaged along the high road and in various directions and in the battle paddock for the next eight minutes. It didn't last as long as many hoped, but *memorable* was the word that some put upon it when they learnt what the word meant.

At about the time the battle ended, Rachel was thirteen years, one month, and three days old, almost through her music lesson in the piano room behind the shop, and about to rush madly home because night was drawing in.

"Nora," came a yell from Sam. "Several young Herberts are bringing in their bodies. They need attention."

"Bother the bodies," cried Miss Nora. "Haven't they got mothers? Rachel's playing Mozart and for once not beating him to death."

"One particular body," yelled Sam, "lives at this address. Its nose is spread from ear to ear. Its mother won't be home till the train comes in."

"I'm sorry about this, dear," Miss Nora said, "but there's not a man about the place can stand the sight of blood. Let's hope they never have a war. Practise your exam piece while I'm gone."

So Rachel sat at the piano with a set expression, not practising her exam piece, or Mozart (whom she *never* beat to death), just tapping one long finger in irritation into middle C. Tapping it so hard that sometimes she sounded the note: a frustrated middle C, then an anxious middle C, then an angry middle C.

"Bother," said Rachel.

Bother was a most excellent way of putting it and that day she appropriated it from Miss Nora and added it to her own vocabulary.

The worst of being a big girl, the worst of being church organist, was that little girls had their lessons first. All the little girls had gone off with their mothers or their aunties. Pitter-patter, chitter-chatter, up the high road or across the high road or round the corner and home having hot buttered toast.

Winter was big trouble.

It was dark so soon. Dark in the sky. Dark on the

ground. Dark inside your own head. Away, away, away into the distance, everywhere dark.

Friday night, too. Everything worse of a Friday. And tonight sounded worse than usual. The high road full of over-excited boys, shouting and screaming, running all over the place. That silly Willie Herbert not ringing the bell. Half the kids of the district whooping it up. Getting along the street was going to be awful, awful.

Summer was marvellous. Well, by comparison. You could see all the way home and the happy beetles clicked and the birds and the cicadas sang and the spooks in the bushlands didn't come out until the door was locked and you were tucked in bed. Safe and sound.

Winter was another world.

Terrible things were always about to happen and sometimes almost did.

Many times she almost heard the hunting cry of the Tantanoola Tiger.

Many times she was almost caught and sold as a captive into Egypt.

A most shocking fate, according to Chrissie Crawford.

"They put you into a harem and you've got to wash the dishes and polish the knives and scrub the floors and carry in the logs for the fire."

"I do that now," said Rachel.

"And there's more," Chrissie said. "You've got to wash all the little kids and put them to bed."

"I do that now," Rachel said.

"And there's more," Chrissie said, "but Eddie won't tell. I'm working on it, though."

An hour's walk it was, between the Herberts' piano and the safe door of the kitchen at home. Or a desperate run. Farther than a racehorse had to go to win the Melbourne Cup. Starting with the full length of town, past all the verandahs and doorways and fences and tree trunks, with cheeky boys leaping out and threatening to pull her pigtails if she didn't give them a kiss.

Imagine kissing those grubby-looking creatures. You'd get foot and mouth disease.

Imagine their poor mothers having to kiss them at bed-time. Perhaps their mothers shook them by the hand and had a good wash afterwards. Perhaps, at prayer time, their mothers said, "Please change Jack into Jill. If you can't manage that please turn him into a ton of firewood or something useful."

Then on past the dreadful hotel full of dreadful drunks who'd been dreadful little boys once upon a time, staggering about the place, being sick all over the road, frightening the life out of her.

Oh goodness, fancy being late on a winter's night, not crossing the paddocks with the usual crowd, girls in one group, boys in the other.

On your own, running, running across the paddocks, miles of blessed paddocks, not a house to be seen, school satchel thudding into your back, knocking the wind and the nerve out of you. Skirting every threatening stand of trees, keeping out in the open away from all the haunted places where men fought and died for gold they never won, shrieking at all the spooks and hoodlums and ruffians you couldn't quite see, "Go away. Go away. Leave me be." Watching out for rabbits and wombats and kangaroos and cowpats and foxes and wild dogs and bulls and the terrible Tiger, thudding across the bridge Dad built over the creek, running up the other side past the duck-pen and the pigsty and the turkey yard and the little house and the woodheap and the chookhouse and Mrs MacArthur and the dairy where the hurricane lamp hung on the post, yelling towards the kitchen window, "Here I am, Auntie Lizzie. Oh, open the door. It's me."

Rachel's long forefinger went on tapping into middle C, a desperate middle C.

Fancy happening tonight, the election tomorrow, Dad hoping to win it, and being a bit superstitious.

"Late?" he'd say. "Ended up in the dark, did you? Out

in the cold, were you? That's not a good omen for me."

Still Miss Nora didn't come and still Willie was wailing somewhere, "No, no, no, I don't want the iodine. Take it away."

On Monday Rachel would be telling the girls that Willie the Ferret was a cry-baby. At the very least!

CHAPTER THREE

The Happy Travellers

At the opening of the side door onto the street, Miss Nora said, "My, that couldn't be the train! We *are* late, aren't we? Where *has* the time gone?"

What are you asking that for? Rachel thought. You're the one that wasted it. Painting that cry-baby with iodine. That horrible cheeky kid. You should've let him bleed. Leaving me to sit. Leaving me to wait. Not caring I had to run all that way home.

"Let's not dawdle then, dear," Miss Nora said. "After all the excitement this afternoon the boys'll be jumping out of their skins if they haven't already been dragged off home. We don't want to be caught in the dark, do we?"

"Oh, no," Rachel said, with a smile so wide, for Miss Nora had said the unbelievable. The beautiful. "Oh, no we don't, Miss Herbert. We don't want to get caught. Oh, thank you, Miss Herbert."

A happy song sang inside Rachel in rhythm to the sounds of the passing train across and beyond the wintry road.

Miss Nora was going to walk her home!

Beautiful Miss Nora. Her face wasn't like a ferret at all. Oh, the smile and the song inside Rachel almost breaking out aloud. Come the dusk, come the dark, let them come. She wouldn't tell on Willie after all.

The door shut.

That slab of wood. The shock of confronting it! The flat face of it. The vastness of it. The brass knocker in the middle of it like a turned-up nose. Miss Herbert cosy on the inside of it. Rachel, back to earth, shivering on the outside of it.

Out in the wild world. Inhabited by savages masquerading as schoolboys. You didn't even have to listen to hear the whoops. Like fun they'd been dragged off home! They were still roving the streets, ready to hide behind trees and jump out of doorways, ready to tease the life out of any girl who dared show her nose.

Where was that awful disappearing policeman? Now you don't have him. Now you still don't have him. You never have him.

Train huffing and chuffing into the station at the bottom end of town blowing its cheery whistle. Barp barp. Here I am, everybody.

All the happy travellers back from Ballarat spilling onto the platform. Doors swinging open and slamming shut. All the happy travellers soon to be walking each other home arm in arm and hand in hand, telling each other of the interesting things they'd seen and done. All the grown-up kids from Continuation School who washed properly every night and didn't smell, the clever ones that were going to be doctors and professors and prime ministers, and the highly intelligent ones that were going to be ladies with gold-rimmed spectacles who didn't have to wash clothes and scrub floors and carry in the logs for the kitchen stove.

Rachel at the top end of town, on her own, all alone, no one to talk to except herself, no hope of going to Continuation School unless Dad struck it rich down that mine and stopped throwing his money down other people's holes in the ground.

Rachel, all alone. Dusk dropping from Heaven like bricks. Evening star coming out in an icy sky. Everywhere cold, everywhere threatening, everywhere absolutely awful, even more terrible than she had feared.

And late. So late. So late.

Miss Nora about to sit in front of her parlour fire and warm her knees and drink her cups of tea and eat piles of lovely hot toast, probably with yellow box honey on.

Rachel about to rush into the wilderness, in fright, on her own, all alone, same as always, same as ever, nothing ever changing. Except that the high road was empty!

She almost doubted her eyes.

North: not a boy to be seen.

South, the critical way, the way home: empty, empty.

Oh my goodness, goodness. Could it really be?

Had those dreadful creatures been dragged away, really, truly, to be soundly whipped and sent to bed without their tea?

Off we go then.

Away she bustled with short, fast, springy, nervous steps like a cat with wet feet trying to shake the drops off, trying to look in all directions just the same.

Home we go. Like the train. On the rails. Signals green. Home for tea. Lovely tea. Cornish pasties, if you please. Tomato sauce, spicy hot, Auntie Lizzie, please. Here comes Rachel. On her own. Very brave. Through the dark, though we'll try to race it home.

Oh, suddenly! Among the boulders on that vacant piece of land, a mob of boys, ten years old, eleven years old, not yet dragged indoors, playing some crazy hysterical game of cannibals and missionaries, prancing round a fire making howling sounds. The whoops she'd heard! The cries! The chanting sounds! Almost as one, they yelled, "There's a juicy chook. We'll have her for the pot."

Rachel's heart all but stopped. Nowhere, anywhere, was there anything looking like a chook but her, and cannibals and missionaries were whooping towards the road waving spears and tomahawks and clubs.

She shrieked.

She fled.

All boys should be locked in cages to the very last one. Why couldn't they stay home and chop wood for their mums?

Nothing human in view. Nothing to save Rachel. The happy travellers were not in sight from the train. No policeman. No company of soldiers. Not even an old lady with an umbrella. No one but the usual helpless drunk weaving his foolish way home.

"You've got a spear in your back," came a howl from behind.

"You're wounded now — yah yah."

"You're dead, sis."

"You've got to fall down."

Rachel rushed past the drunk who waved his walking cane as if about to strike her on the head.

"Scabby rabble," the drunk shouted. "Get thee off to your residences." Which meant the drunk was Ole Roll heading for his hut the wrong way. There'd surely be nowhere else for him to go.

Crack went the cane. Rachel heard it strike bone, mercifully not her own.

"The doctor be her father and he'll leave thee to die of the rots!"

Crack went the cane and Rachel looked behind. Cannibals and missionaries were scattering, were shrieking, "Lay off, Ole Roll, silly old fool. You'll kill someone, silly old fool. The doctor hasn't got a daughter."

Swish went the cane.

"Then the policeman be her father and he'll lock thee up on bread and water once a day."

"He'll lock you up, stinkin' Ole Roll. Yah yah. The policeman's daughters are grown-up ladies with babies."

"Then the priest be her father and he'll commit the lot of thee to hell."

Swish went the cane, though not a boy was near.

"Be off with you, young lady. This is no hour to be abroad and tell your father I said so."

Swish went the cane.

"Filthy little snots. Get thee off to your residences and

wipe your dirty noses. Be gone with you, young Rachel. Do I still see you there or am I to presume you're a pro- vocatrix and a shame upon your calling?"

"I don't think so, sir. On Tuesdays and Fridays I'm a pianist. On Sundays I'm an organist."

"Of that I'm well aware!"

"My music finished late, sir, and I had to wait while Miss Herbert put iodine on Willie's nose."

"Go," cried the drunk, "for darkness presses all around."

Swish went the cane in Rachel's direction, so she called in parting, "Thank you, sir, but if you're heading for home, please do go the other way or you'll end up in the cold. It was very nice of you to take care of me. My father, Mr Frank Lefevre, will be much obliged."

"I know who your father is and I may yet convey my word directly to his ear."

To herself Rachel said, I hope he's got some sense in his head, this Ole Roll. You can smell the frost in the air, or is it whisky or beer?

Now all the happy travellers were visible on the road coming away from the train. Hooray. And off had gone the train, chuffing round through the hills towards the next station far down the line. Now all those gangs of abominable boys would have to tease each other or go without their entertainment, for who would persecute girls or throw stones while crowds of grown-ups passed by with bull-sized voices and man-sized hands? A reprieve, of a kind.

Rachel bustled down the centre of the road, satchel swinging, past the town church where they had two grown-up organists, one for the morning, the other for night. "No better than you, though," Dad said.

"How would you know, Dad? You've never heard them."

"Don't need to, love."

Marvellous, having an admiration society at home.

Dad was blessed with a musical sense so strong he'd not allow himself to sing a note in public. If a fellow couldn't stand the sound of his own voice something had to be wrong with it.

Past Kane's General Store.

Outside, the sandwich board that said:

> Today's Bargain
> Direct from Norway
> Smoked sardines 5½ d.

Rachel adored sardines. On toast. On bread. Out of the tin. Fancy sticking that notice almost in the middle of the road when she was running so late.

Past Kane's Coaching Stables.

Inside, the coach horses, feasting, home in the crib, safe and sound, noses stuffed into feedbags, gorging.

Past the public hall.

The notice board nailed to the wall:

> Magic Lantern Lecture and Demonstration
> Friday 14 July 8.30 p.m.
> Mrs Ernest Headstrong of Sacramento.USA
> *Your Future in Your Bumps*
> Adults 9d. Children 4½ d.
> Profits to Hall Committee
> Bring a Supper Plate.

This very night, but Rachel didn't have time to read the notice again and brood over it. She knew it was sending out its signals as she hurried by.

Why aren't you coming, Rachel, to see the lovely lady and hear the lovely lecture and watch the lovely pictures? Don't you want to know about the future? Don't you want to know whether you're going to be famous? Don't you care?

Grumble, grumble.

What's wrong with Dad? And Chrissie's dad? Always dying on a principle. Both staying away and keeping their families away. Miserable things. Because Chrissie's dad couldn't stand Hamish Herbert and reckoned no hall was big enough to hold the both of them. And Rachel's dad couldn't stand Councillor Dave Hobson, even before he started circulating all those terrible lies specially for the Election, the theme of his campaign being *Desperate Days Begin When Frank Lefevre Walks In*.

Yes. And after the lecture, lovely supper with cream cakes and coffee and buttered nut loaves.

Another notice on the notice board, known by heart, sending out its signals to echo in her head as she bustled away:

Council Elections East Riding
Candidates:
Cr David E. Hobson & Mr Francis J. Lefevre Jnr.
Ratepayers vote here Saturday 15 July
8 a.m. to 6 p.m.
George P. Hobson, Shire Secretary.

If Dad won, life'd never be the same. He'd be the *dignitary* instead of that big ape Hobson. Dad's sister Lizzie and his kids would be *dignitaries*. Councillor Francis John Lefevre Junior and family.

And one notice more was left behind, back there on the board:

Warning
Any person caught messing about
with this notice board
will be severely manhandled by
Hamish Herbert, Secretary, Hall Committee.

Rachel rushing past all the little shops, even past the barber, where that awful Mr Basset brandished a razor in his bandaged right hand. Serve him right. Perhaps he'd slipped.

Then past Miss Harriet Hobson's Haberdashery Shoppe with the Nottingham lace in the window, a matter of continuing interest to Rachel because once she had made a purchase there.

Then past the post office where Mrs Clarrie Crawford

sold the loveliest treacle sticks in the world, if you were legally able to buy one. Regrettably an infrequent event.

Then past the pub.

Rachel at once crossed over and hurried by on the opposite side, as far away from it as she could get without stumbling through the ditch or climbing the fence. Looking directly ahead as every well-brought-up young lady was expected to do. Not even glancing across to the wide-open doorway for the briefest glimpse of the degradation there. Nor permitting her ears to hear it, blocking them off inside with the sounds of stirring temperance hymns. Unhappily, at the last moment, forgetting to pinch her nostrils and catching the infamous undiluted drift of it.

Oh, the shock of it, the smell of it, of all those awful men paddling round ankle-deep in the spillage of it.

Rachel hurried faster, faster, creaking for air, trying to exist without it, but with the first desperate breath the drift hit her again like a collision.

They ought to burn the place down. Truly. Truly. Front door. Back door. Everything in the middle. Then they ought to shovel the lot down the deepest mine shaft and jump on it.

All the happy travellers coming from the train had gone from the road.

Oh.

Suddenly, they'd shut their doors and were inside, safe, warm, not to be seen, stoking their fires and having lovely tea and hot buttered toast. Perhaps having spare ribs, if anyone round about had killed a pig of late. Perhaps having pea soup. Perhaps having Heinze's sausages brought home from Ballarat. And Rachel was all alone, on her own, out in the dusk, out in the cold, same as ever, nothing to eat, night getting ready to fall on top of her like a ton weight.

Running again, on down that long road until she came to the short cut and the paddocks were lying on the other side, stretching into gloom, and over to the right, on the low side, were dark bushlands where rough young fellows of bad reputation had their hiding places.

"Though it's shorter," Dad said, "never go through the bush."

Life was an endless complication.

And over to the left, on the high side, were more dark bushlands, where she'd never set foot, and from which she veered away to the right, always, as far as she dared.

"Never in there," Dad said. "The Devil's Hot Pot runs its gullies back through there. To say nothing of the mine shafts no one's ever filled. That post-and-rail fence is intended to keep the cattle out. And to keep children out. And to remind grown-ups to keep out. Do you hear me, Rachel?"

She heard.

The sliprail.

She plunged under and came out running, satchel whacking into her back, dusk deepening, and cold coming down as if the ice maidens were sweeping out their icy rooms and shaking out their icy mats.

"I'm going to get my nose freezed off. Then it'll rain, like it always rains when I'm late. I'll get soaked. I'll get pneumonia and they'll send the hearse away with ostrich plumes on it and all the people tracking behind. . .

"Then they'll say, 'Fancy that lovely girl, fancy that wonderful hymn player, fancy that brilliant girl who makes up her own voluntaries, fancy that generous-hearted, sweet-natured girl who tops her class at school when the clever ones get the chicken pox, fancy her left dying in the rain, left dead in the icy paddock, because Willie Herbert was late with the bell and got his nose bashed and the high road was left full of yelling hoodlums jumping out of their skins. But for that the lovely Rachel could've hurried home in daylight, safe and sound, and she wouldn't have been snatched from us like a half-grown apple from the bough, and we wouldn't have had to go to this sad funeral when there aren't any flowers except dried ones in glass cases and everything's such a slush you've got to put rocks in the coffin to make it sink to the bottom of the hole.'"

It was terrible the things that might happen to Rachel.

"I wish my dad would come running up the paddock: 'Rachel, Rachel, here I am.'

"I wish my dad wasn't down that mine and going nowhere till a quarter past six.

"I wish I was home in front of our kitchen stove eating hot buttered toast.

"I wish silly Willie Herbert hadn't got his stupid nose squashed.

"I don't know what boys see in it. Always bashing and bruising and bleeding. Always falling out of trees on their heads. Always tumbling down mine shafts. As if the big thing in life was to get killed yesterday. Always teasing me. Always pulling my hair. No wonder my hair's halfway down to my feet."

Rachel ran and ran, her nose turning colder and colder, her chin going numb, her breathing coming faster and sharper as if those wretched ice maidens were tipping the icicles straight down her throat. But oh my goodness no, lower down, where the cows were!

Rearing between her and home like the heads of hunters rising from cover, a gang of boys! Yes. Yes. Or else they came into view. Boys in a fever like the rest of them. Silly season for boys.

She'd always known that one winter's night, as dark came dropping from the sky, terrible things would stop happening in her head and start happening all around.

First, in fright, she saw three. Then worse, there were five. A pack. A pack.

Boys hunting in a pack, out to frighten old people sick, out to terrorise gangs of kids smaller than themselves, out to scare young girls half to death.

"Riff-raff," she'd heard Carter Hooke roar at them on

the right-hand side of the room, banging one fist into the other. "Hoodlums. Mindless louts. Rabble. Give me an honest savage any day."

"Oh, no," Rachel cried, and somehow kept her weakening legs heading for the dark bushlands on the top side where she was supposed never to go. There was no other way, no other refuge. Only the dark bushlands with the shafts and the rifts and the gullies. Inevitable somehow.

Out in front, the unattainable track home, a long, long track of downhill and uphill and over and under fences and along the winding creek. The only house closer than home, Crawford's, where Chrissie and Eddie lived, and that wasn't closer by much.

Were there really five pairs of long legs stretching out behind? And five strident voices? Not imagined? Happening in the real world, but like the worst dream?

What did she want to learn music for?

Why couldn't she wake up one morning and know it all?

The fence!

She crashed into it.

CHAPTER FOUR

White Plumes for the Young

Forty years old, that post-and-rail fence at the edge of the bushlands, as solid as tree trunks.

Rachel crashed into it as if she'd not known it was there, immediately recoiling and launching herself between the rails, furiously, wrenching her caught-up satchel after her, thrusting into the bushland on the other side, away from the open places, into the dark and forbidden places.

Madly.

"You're never to go in there," Dad said. "It's unsafe. It's bad."

For once Dad was wrong. There was nowhere else. Was she to allow them to stop her head-on or run her down?

Trees were dark ahead, were massed, were shapeless. Darkness like clouds moved in her vision, or else in her head. Darkness that was jagged and scratched at her, though everything looked featureless, blunt and huge, like the sides of elephants.

She ran, stunned and stinging and short of breath, dragging her snared clothing free, snatching herself back from everything that caught at her, as if wildness alone might protect her.

"It's a dangerous place," Dad said.

Oh, she knew that, for she was exhausted and scattered and scared, hedged about by rifts and channels, by the perilous edges of the Hot Pot that could have been any-

33

where, unseen. It was a dead end, the Rachel pit, the Rachel trap.

Night was so much nearer here, as if darkness were barely seconds away, in wait, as if darkness lived here and brooded here and reached out into all the world when evening came.

Shafts were everywhere around like eruptions of boils, a fevered confusion, a hostility, a desolation of diggings abandoned long ago, so close to the wide green fields, to the open run home.

The ground around was white, a ghostly white quartz rubble like old bones, or grey-white, or a kind of black-white, slippery with the lichens of years.

It was a terrible thing she had done. A terrible haste. A terrible unthinking.

She could have fallen here. A broken leg or a sprained ankle. Oh, so easily. So lucky so far she'd not.

"You mustn't go in there," Dad said. "Ever."

He was so right. You couldn't escape in here. All the chaos of the past crowded about you. You could feel it. There were ghosts. They were beside you.

The gullies were a maze that could take you deeper and deeper until there were high cliffs and huge boulders always about to fall, and below were dark caves where the captives of the devil were chained.

They had done this to her, those boys.

Boys in a band like brigands out on the scare.

Why was it that boys made sport of girls?

Did you ever find boys at the Misses Herbert learning piano? Only the small boys, misbehaving, driving Miss Nora or Miss Sarah mad, until they turned into big boys and joined the gangs out on the scare.

She bent in despair, ribs sore as if they were about to fold inside her, afraid to move.

You could go so far and then no farther. You could stand so much and then you had to wait for it. In this terrible place. Forty years ago the grown-ups put the fence

across the face of it, yet the fence was behind her instead
of in front.

No one came.

Her perspiration turned clammy, then chill, and from
every clammy spot the chill spread.

The sound of the heartbeat running wild in her
head began to quieten. There were bird sounds again,
currawongs. Then she felt the cold in the ground and in
the air, as great as the chill within herself.

Every muscle and nerve went on shaking.

There wasn't a human sound except an axeman far
away splitting wood.

"Oh, axeman, why aren't you here?"

Then farther away a fragment of a woman's call to
children out of doors. Perhaps Auntie Lizzie calling
Rennie, calling Rose. Inside they'd go and shut the door.
The cooking stove hot. The lamps lit.

Or was it Auntie Lizzie calling, "Rachel. Rachel. Are
you there? Hurry on. Dark's coming."

She sank back on her heels on the rough ground and
began to cry, stifling the sound, fearing that the boys
might be stalking her still and then would stand off in the
gloom, looking vague and ruthless like Vikings, as if they
gave no thought to the fears and pains of others.

She'd not be able to see their faces, but she knew the
corners of their mouths would be twisting.

They'd say, "What are you blubbing for, sis? What
grade are you in at school? The blubs?"

It was terribly cold.

Mother died of cold.

Rachel heard her die in the night. Rachel aged five.

She heard the sounds of pneumonia taking Mother
away.

One moment Mother was there as she had been from
the moment that Rachel's world began. The next
moment there was a cry, a man's cry, and everyone in the
house was alone.

The hearse went away with white ostrich plumes bending and bowing. Black plumes for old people; white plumes for young.

Everyone except the children walking or riding behind, all the way to the cemetery round by the road.

Mother was gone.

Rachel was alone then, and now.

"Keep out of that place," Dad said. "It was bad when I was a boy and that was long ago. Two boys I knew; they walked in; they never walked out. No place for girls to be."

She pushed the thought away; pushed it down. Two boys walking in, never walking out. No white plumes for them; no bodies found.

White plumes for Rachel? She pushed the thought down, down.

A ridiculous, terrible, foolish thing she had done.

"You in there! Hey, girl! Come on out!"

Her heart leapt and she started up as if to flee, but where? Every way was dark, was solid, was impassable. Every way looked like that, but wasn't. It'd let you through, let you in, but would never let you out.

"Hey, you in there. Do you hear?"

How far off were they? Or how near?

Her breath burnt again.

The direction of the call had changed. It had an edge, a breaking edge, and came quietly, intensely, as if held back, as if held down, perhaps so that people at a distance wouldn't hear.

Rachel said, murmuring, "Why don't you come for me, Dad? Why must you be down that mine and so far away?"

"You can't stay in there. It's dangerous in there. Do you hear?"

It was the same voice, the same boy, but another new direction. Perhaps the voice was turning corners. Perhaps the boy was running up and down the line of the fence, as a dog might do, trying to break out or break in.

"*Please. Do you hear me? Come out.*"

No.

She'd been teased too many times. Teased on the way to school. Teased in the school ground. Teased on the way home. Was there a girl who hadn't been?

She sat on her heels, flinching, trying to make herself impossible to find.

Rachel said, murmuring, "I can't go through this any more. It's the very last time. I'll have to teach myself music at home out of books. Or you'll have to teach me, Auntie Lizzie. Or Dad, you'll have to try."

"*I'm coming in to get you out, girl. Don't you run off again. You'll fall down a shaft. You'll die.*"

She tried to close him off, tried not to listen, but he went on, sometimes shrill, sometimes hoarse.

"*What did you want to run in there for? You're mad. You're crazy. Give me a call so I know you're not down a shaft already.*"

His voice was breaking, but she made no reply.

"*I'll never find you if you don't help.*"

She wished he'd go away.

"*Come out by yourself then, but come out careful. The ground gives way.*"

She waited a minute, or two, or longer, and thought at last he'd gone — the relief of it — but it wasn't to be.

He was calling again.

"*If you don't tell me you're all right, I'll have to get my dad, and you know what that'll mean. We'll have to come with dogs and lights and ropes. Are you trying to get me into trouble? You know his temper.*"

Oh. She knew all right. Knew the man's temper, and knew the boy.

The shock. The amazement. The hurt.

How could Eddie Crawford be in a gang out on the scare?

Eddie... Eddie gone mad.

Did anyone ever tease when Eddie joined the crowd on the way back or forth to school? There wasn't a kid who'd dare.

Eddie... Eddie in a fever. The silly season for boys.

"You're being real mean, Rachel, and real stupid, running away. For gawd's sake, why?"

All the time Eddie had known, chasing after her, shouting at her, frightening the life out of her.

Eddie... At heart a hoodlum like them all.

On Sundays he sat in the front row near the organ looking at her for longer than was properly polite, bringing colour to her cheeks. Well, everyone knew. Everyone could see. People weren't blind. They knew Eddie fancied her. They knew she didn't know how to handle it, but they knew she didn't mind.

Dad said, "Don't go falling in love with Eddie Crawford."

"Oh, *Dad*."

"Crawfords everywhere, love, even when I was a kid. I fancied Cassie. Would you blame me? Fancied Clarrie, too. My dad didn't approve. He was right. I'm right, too. Crawfords everywhere, breeding their heads off, aimin' on populating the planet. Should've called the place Crawfordsville. Or Herbertsville. Or Hobsonsville. At the present rate of increase it might have made sense to call the country Crawfordalia."

"Oh, *Dad*, I don't care about boys. There isn't a boy in town that's not dead ordinary."

Was this what Dad meant? There were problems, he said, when people were too close.

"Finding anyone to marry, Rachel, round here, for anyone growing up here, is getting very hard. Everyone's too close. I went off to Melbourne when I felt the urge. Thanks to Auntie Susie, it's where I found your mother, Auntie Susie's friend. And where had she come from? Hundreds and hundreds of miles in the opposite direction. In time I'll be making sure you do the same.

Friendships round here have got to be short term."

"You're making too much of it, Dad."

"I grew up, too, Rachel. Don't forget I'm your father. They're all too close, these people. All the Crawfords. All the Hobsons. All the Herberts."

But there was a boy in town who wasn't ordinary, just the same.

He was calling with a low voice, frightened and earnest.

"You're being awful. You're not being fair. All those rotten kids have scooted off home."

Her very own best friend's very own brother. Chrissie's very own favourite brother.

She'd choke if she answered him.

When she saw him again she'd walk off.

When he looked her way in church she'd ignore him. Her face white, she'd turn the music pages as if he wasn't there.

People would come to the organ and say, "Are you sick, dear? Are you all right?"

She despised Eddie Crawford in a gang on the scare.

Eddie kept bantams and pigeons and built proper houses for them, safe houses, tight enough to keep out the foxes and the rain. He built his mum a shoebox with a hinged lid that didn't fall off. He was different from the others. He made things. Good things. He cared. He made Chrissie a clothes rack with polished knobs. *David Copperfield* was his very favourite book. It was Rachel's favourite, too. And he was learning to play the bagpipes as his father and grandfather had done before him, even if the wail across the countryside sent little children rushing indoors. "Is it Eddie or the Tantanoola Tiger?"

Eddie called again, an anguished cry. *"Rachel..."*

It was night then and quite dark, quite still, quite cold. A black and sparkling sky was up there, but didn't give the light Rachel needed to see by.

She'd never find her way alone.

Eddie said to be careful or the ground might move. Nervously, she reached out a hand.

Eddie said he'd have to get his dad and they'd come with lights, and dogs, and ropes. Then there'd be trouble of another kind.

"Don't ever let me hear you've been in there," Dad said.

"As if I would, Dad. As if I ever would."

She was in the middle of it and she'd sent Eddie away, and they'd both be in awful trouble, and it all went back to Willie Herbert's nose.

"Eddie!"

She heard her own despairing cry.

"Eddie Crawford, I'm here."

Her voice wasn't strong enough, didn't have the body or the breath.

"Eddie!"

He'd gone out of hearing, beyond the reach of a bigger voice than hers, and his going was her own doing. Eddie had gone home to tell his dad. And that was the worst thing he could do. He was a terrible bad-tempered fellow, that father of Chrissie's, that father of Eddie's. And the other boys had run away, like big tough swaggering fellows, leaving Eddie, like Rachel, to face the music on his own, to take the blame.

"Eddie!"

No axeman now. No birds now. No fragments of a distant voice that might have been Auntie Lizzie. Everyone's door was shut. Every kid's day was over. Auntie Lizzie and the lighted kitchen window were in a warm, glowing, safe place, where Rennie and Rose were toasting homemade bread on long black forks on the glowing coals of the stove.

And Dad was down the mine.

Where had she put herself? On ground that moved in the deep sinking cold.

A moment's madness, of panic, and it was done.

"*Rachel!*"

She was on her feet, suddenly, reaching, as if to hold to the call.

"It's me. I'm Rachel. Yes, I am. Here. Here."

The call had gone as if slipping from her hands.

"I answered," Rachel shrieked. "Didn't you hear?"

How puny her voice must have been. But there were new sounds, faintly, a rumble of wheels, horses' hooves on flint-hard quartz, driver whistling — faraway sounds travelling mysteriously through rifts and gullies and folds in the land.

"*Rachel, do you hear me?*"

"Yes, yes, yes."

"*Are you down a hole or something?*"

"No!"

"*Do you hear the coach?*"

"Yes, yes."

"*Tell me if you see the lights?*"

Masses of darkness were all around, as if the masses moved.

"No lights!"

"*Are they near or far?*"

"I said I didn't see the lights."

"*Don't you move. Which direction? Where did you see them?*"

"I didn't see them!"

"*Oh Lord. Don't move.*"

"I'm not moving!"

"*You're an idiot, Rachel, running in here.*"

It was true. An idiot. And the coach had gone out of hearing on towards the Crawford house, on towards Rachel's house, on down the gully road, driver probably still whistling his carefree tune, a heap of Ballarat afternoon newspapers beside him for flicking at gateposts along the way. Nothing else to claim his attention except the dark road ahead. No hold-ups at this time of day. Nothing to hold him up for, except for letters to Miss May

Herbert and Master Jack Hobson and Mrs Edna
Crawford and who'd hold anyone up for those?

Rachel should have hailed him in town. "Please,
Mr Driver. Take me home. Dad'll pay." But how could
she have known he'd been delayed and hadn't gone
through an hour ago.

Darkness everywhere. Everywhere the same.

"*Are you there, Rachel?*"

"I haven't moved."

Eddie's low, careful voice seemed closer.

He wasn't coming with lights and he wasn't coming
with his dad.

"*Rachel, whistle a tune.*"

"I can't whistle."

"*Everyone can whistle.*"

"I don't. I can't."

"*Sing then.*"

"What've I got to sing about?"

"*So I can find you. Sing la-la-la or something. You've
got to guide me.*"

"I can't sing la-la-la standing here on my own."

"*Would you rather they found you dead?*"

"La-la-la," she sang, in a frail little voice. Then a
few more la-la's that sounded something like the tune of
"Nearer My God to Thee".

"*Sing up. All the playing you do. Can't you hold a
tune?*"

"Playing's different from singing," she said, to herself,
for Eddie couldn't have heard.

"*Sing something I can hear. Open your mouth. Bellow.*"

"I can't," Rachel said, and sang "God Save the King",
but in the middle forgot the words, as never in her life
before, no words, no tune, only the cold air burning her
throat.

She seemed to be slipping into a huddle again and
somewhere Eddie was calling intensely, "*Sing up. Where
are you?*"

She made no answer.

The cold was in her brain, taking her away from the present, to a safe place.

CHAPTER FIVE

Rush of Blood

They were in the buggy; an impossibility; she knew the buggy wasn't there, but she was in it just the same.

The beautiful buggy, jolting, juddering — a dizzying excitement — and the road was rolling invisibly underneath and Rose with all her might was blowing the horn that Rachel gave her for Christmas. Well, with as much might as a small girl has at five years of age when it's half-past three in the morning.

At bedtime who could've guessed that Dad's voice was to rouse them out of the deep dark?

"All hands on deck. It's half-past two o'clock and your clothes are laid out beside you and your breakfast's on the table and the ship sails in forty-five minutes precisely."

Everyone in a fuddle. Rachel immediately walking into the wall and bumping her nose. The blue night-light already turned up and a yellow light held by Auntie Lizzie coming in through the doorway, Auntie Lizzie saying, "Happy Christmas. Your clothes are beside you. Lovely warm kitchen waiting. Lovely scrambled eggs. Lovely hot cocoa. Lovely hot buttered toast. Father Christmas has been, though nothing's to be seen, and no child may utter a word or the spell may break and Christmas may fail to take its unexpected turn."

"It's a great big bunch of daisies," Dad called from the next room, "exciting the eye and pleasing the heart, but silence is the rule as you've heard."

Understanding that lady or that fellow in the middle of the night was difficult. They were terrible people, the things they did with words.

Then sitting at the kitchen table in the warm yellow light, blinking across the expanse of it, catching one pair of eyes, then another, feeling a bit sick in the tum, for if Father Christmas had called on those who were young enough to expect him, he had left no evidence. Rachel couldn't even see the things she had put out for the family. Perhaps they'd been spirited on to the Hobsons next door who might have had the greater need.

Grumble, grumble.

Fancy getting bundled out of bed when you can't see a thing and banging your nose on the wall. And Rennie putting her feet in the wrong boots and Rose falling down the step into the kitchen and no one brave enough to say a word except "*Ow*," for if spells really were drifting about the house. . . It was nonsense. It was rubbish. But you had to be careful, just in case!

Two minutes to three by the clock under the shot-gun and you knew you weren't dreaming any more, even though it was the wrong time for lovely hot cocoa and lovely scrambled eggs and lovely hot toast oozing with potted butter, but the right time for feeling so confused that your heart was jumping all over the place — well, if you were ten like Rachel.

If you were five like Rose, you were pale and dull-eyed and yawning. Or if you were just eight like Rennie you were looking very serious and worrying whether this had something to do with that ear doctor fellow in Ballarat, because Auntie Lizzie was cutting sandwiches.

Dad put his mug of tea aside and said, "The Crawfords'll be feeding the birds and animals and milking the cow for us. We're going to be on the road all day, going away, a great distance."

What an incredible thing to happen to Christmas Day!

Dad said, in his maddening way of hardly ever getting to the point in anything straighter than a crooked line, "You may ask why it's necessary to take this journey so unexpectedly on Christmas Day?"

Rachel knew that Rennie was thinking, Yes, I'd like the answer very soon. But it doesn't take a day to drive to Ballarat. And don't we leave after the sun's come up?

"Well," said Dad, "a week or two ago Rachel won five shillings in the music competition at Cambridge Reef. Everyone in the family knows she should've come first and won ten shillings. Other people have expressed the same opinion. Everyone knows that the girl who took out the big prize takes piano lessons from the judge. That's life. But we keep our feelings private. We don't want to be known as bad losers."

A real funny time to be discussing music competitions and the rights and wrongs of losing.

"In a few minutes," Dad said, "we're about to learn that Rachel spent nothing of her prize on herself. The only sum like it she's ever had and it all went on presents for us."

Rachel blushed and lowered her eyes. There'd been no sacrifice. It had been *fun* choosing the presents, an *excitement* paying.

"*Rachel!*"

Eddie was just over the edge somewhere. At the fringe of consciousness.

Dad was smiling. Grinning, really. A grin that went on growing wider as he said, "It's fairly well known round this house that I can't take a holiday, but it might be asked why should everyone else have to stay home year after year? Rachel's action set me thinking. So you're going to find Billy and Larry harnessed up in the buggy outside, waiting there, would you believe, when Father Christmas rushed by dropping off a few items on his way. Each of you then, out you go, into your usual seats. It's the seaside you're heading for, for the first time in your lives..."

Away they drove into the night, heading south, the journey of half a night and a whole day ahead of them, Auntie Lizzie clutching her Nottingham lace handkerchief from Miss Harriet Hobson's Haberdashery Shoppe, Dad with a fingertip touching at his tie-pin, Rennie discussing names for her doll with the china face, Rose blowing her horn with all her might, and Rachel glowing with a gilt-edged copy of *The Wide, Wide World* by Elizabeth Wetherell.

"*Rachel!*"

Eddie didn't mean her to remain in that beautiful buggy. Dad wasn't really there with his gun under the seat, and the road wasn't rolling underneath, and that Christmas morning was long ago, that magic morning, hardly another morning like it ever.

"*Rachel!*"

Go away, Eddie Crawford. I don't need you round here. I want our beautiful buggy back again. I want our journey across the sun-coloured countryside all the way to the sea. No pain then. Life on a crest. Picnics at the roadside, every few hours. Arriving at nightfall at the guesthouse, Venus bright and white over the glassy sea. Only one shadow; knowing that Dad would be starting back again next morning, going home, going alone.

"*Rachel!*"

Eddie seemed close, much too close, as if close enough to touch and her anger against him returned with a rush of blood.

"Chah!"

"Is that you, Rachel?"

"Chah!"

"I thought you were the Tiger!"

There was Eddie, near, making a vague shape like a clown in a world of darkness. Suited him to perfection.

"Tiger, my big toe!"

"I'm sorry about all this," he said.

"*Sorry!*"

She choked up with indignation and leapt at him and struck him several times in the chest with all her strength. And he was past fourteen and no weakling. And she was just a little thing. She'd never hit anyone in anger before. Surprising how satisfying it was.

"I detest you, Eddie Crawford."

She'd have run from him then, if there'd been anywhere to run. Perhaps he'd have run from her, too, but he took the blows, grunting.

Her fists fell to her sides, her breath gone.

He said, "Look, I'm really sorry. I never thought you'd take fright."

She hissed at him.

"You're an idiot rushing in here," he said passionately. "You're mad. After everything we've been told. What d'you think the fence is there for? You're mad." He was angry, exasperated, and frightened. "We were only going to walk you home. Well, I was going to. They were only there for the start."

"Chah."

"You know every one of us. Running from us as if we were a gang or something. I know you get scared. Why shouldn't I walk you home when you're scared?"

She shrilled, "You're the one that scared me. Hoodlum. Bully boy. Roving the countryside. Hunting in a pack. Your dad'll kill you."

"We weren't in a pack! We were on our way home after the fight and looking out for you, till I decided you must've been coming along behind getting later and getting scareder."

"I don't believe you, Eddie Crawford. You're just trying to make things fit."

"I'm *not* trying to make things fit. There's nothing to fit when you're telling the truth."

"If you wanted to walk me home sometime there were ways. You could've asked permission of my dad. You see him every Sunday. He only lives next door. You could've got Chrissie to ask at least."

"I suppose that rotten Miss Herbert left you for dead, didn't she? I suppose she went off to stick Willie together again and forgot all about you, didn't she?"

"She couldn't let him bleed all over the house! If any-one's to blame it's the boy who bashed him."

Eddie breathed out very heavily because in a round-about way it had to be true.

"Calling me *girl* as if you didn't know who it was. What was the point? Hoping I'd come on out on my own, then you could hide so I wouldn't see you and would never know. I reckon I despise you, Eddie Crawford. I reckon it's going to take me a month to believe it."

His sigh was close to desperation. "I know it doesn't look good."

"It'll never look good."

"It wasn't that way."

"Saying it's easy."

"You know I'd never do anything to hurt you and if anyone else tried I'd smash 'em."

"I used to think that."

"I'm losing all ways," Eddie cried. Then he stopped.

She felt the stop. Felt the change in the air. But she wasn't ready to make peace. There was a cost he hadn't met.

In a deliberate voice he said, "Getting out of here. That's what we should be worrying about. I don't know how it's happened. I can't believe it. But I'm trying to get used to the idea. If we don't get out of here very quickly we'll be in terrible trouble."

"You found me, didn't you?"

"Finding you was a fluke."

There was a fear in him, and it was contagious.

"Flukes have nothing to do with getting out," he said. "There you were. All of a sudden. Calling you, calling you. And there you were. What were you doing? Calling you and you wouldn't answer. Scaring me sick. In such a funk you couldn't even croak. Down on your knees prayin' to yourself. Give me your hand."

My goodness, how she wanted to, but she said, "I

wouldn't give you my hand, Eddie Crawford, if you were the first prize. You're the real booby prize."

"Look, Rachel. We've got to start playing on the same side. If you won't give me your hand, at least have the brains to follow on behind. How many times have I got to say I'm sorry? But you made a mistake, too."

"Coming home minding my own business. Running like mad because my music was late, because of Willie's nose... You'd better not tell me you blooded it."

"Oh gawd," moaned Eddie.

"So you *are* telling me!"

He moaned. "Someone had to do it."

"Getting chased by you and a gang of hoodlums. And you're even the one that blooded his nose! You tell me what mistake I made! And where are the lights you were bringing?"

"I didn't bring them, did I?"

"What about your dad? Where's he?"

"I didn't bring him either. I didn't tell him, did I? And don't you tell him."

"I won't have to tell him. Chrissie'll do that."

"You leave my sister out of it."

"I'll leave out and put in whoever I please."

He took a very noisy breath. "Do you know this is the only time we've ever talked on our own! Not even Chrissie listening in, with her big ears. I've been waitin' for it for ages. But now I think I've had enough. I think I'll leave you right here."

"I don't care. I'll find my way."

He took a few steps, while her heart leapt wildly. A few steps only.

Thank goodness. Oh dear oh dear. Boys were very complicated, it seemed. Like girls. She'd thought boys were simple things. Like clockwork. If you wound them up they'd go through the same motions every time. But they didn't.

"All right," she said. "I'm coming."

She felt so critical of herself. Even wondered if her anger was a performance, a bit like Sundays at the organ, hoping for everybody to hear and to know.

Eddie had heard by now. He knew.

She shuffled almost into contact.

"I'm here." Then said more, despite herself, "Though I could get out on my own, of course, if I wanted to."

Eddie was breathing hard, was sighing, was restless, or torn, as if trying to head off in several directions at once, as if caught up in some sort of storm.

Rachel thought, he's mad with me. Really, really, I've said enough. If he leaves me here on my own, what *will* I do?

Silence.

Waiting on Eddie.

Then he said, "Gee, Rachel. . . I'm not proud of myself. I'm just so sorry you got frightened. And your dad's just so scared if you get a bad fright you'll drop dead. That's what he tells my dad. That's what my dad tells me. Take care of Rachel, he says. Keep a real friendly eye on her, he says. She's a real frail flower. Here today, gone tomorrow, he says. I could've killed you of fright."

"My dad said that about me? Everyone saying that about me?"

My goodness, she thought. A frail flower. Like a day lily. Here today. Gone tomorrow. Me? Is that what my dad thinks of me? I don't think that's nice.

"If I'd used my brains," Eddie said, "I would've known you'd panic. Maybe any girl would've. It was a terrible thing I did, chasing after you. Stupid, stupid thing to do. It's because of me we're in here. Not because of you. I knew you'd be late. I knew you'd be scared running through. . . Don't know how many times I've watched you go through. . . I said to the kids. . . Oh, it doesn't matter what I said. . . How could I expect them to hang around after you panicked? They were only helping out so I could walk you home. But I wish they hadn't left me to it.

Leaving us here on our own. This is a terrible place to be. Gee, Rachel, I wish you hadn't picked this place. The other way would've been better. Oh gawd, so much better than here. . . In the dark. . . We're out on a limb. Out on the very end. . ."

Timidly she said, "You came through here, down into the Hot Pot, before you were nine."

"What you do now, and what you did then; they're different, Rachel. Getting out of here tonight mightn't be on. Might be too dangerous. Getting in was lucky. Real lucky. Real lucky stars, shining on you, shining on me. Trying to get out of here we could die. What way's out? I don't know. Do you? The Devil's Hot Pot. We might be on the edge of it. All those rough fellows down there. I can't bash them if they get rough. I wouldn't even fancy my brothers in a fight with them. I think we've got to sit the night out. I do. Being quiet. That jolly Tiger, too. We've got to wait till they come to us, Rachel. The whole town'll be out searching soon. We're wiped out. They won't let us within half a mile of each other again. I'll never live it down. Not my dad being the way he is."

Rachel took a hold on Eddie's arm, just briefly, to let him know she understood, though she was not wholly sure that she did.

CHAPTER SIX

Fall of the Hero

Eddie had gone silent. Like a curtain fall. Like an ending.

There he was. Beside her. His height. His presence. His strength. But Eddie was different from what she'd thought him to be. The breaks in his voice. The breathlessness.

Imagine Eddie being scared. Of anything!

Was he scared of the dark or of his dad's big hand?

"It's dark in here, black dark in here, for another thirteen hours," he said as if to himself. "What are we doing here? We've got to keep warm."

"Frost," she said.

Eddie sighed. "We need a shelter. Under a tree at least." But he made no move.

The trees were up there. The branches. The leaves. The stars. Clear, bright stars. Frost getting ready to happen.

They had to play on the same side, Eddie said. She'd do that.

Everything so quiet. Like a dead world.

That lovely seaside holiday. All the ladies and gentlemen in bright colours, in broad stripes like ornamental convicts, running in and out of the warm water.

No.

Rennie falling off the Esplanade, tripping over her big toe, landing in the middle of someone else's picnic.

No.

Other times and other places had to go. It had to be now, with the Devil's Hot Pot over there — or perhaps there. And the bad men. And that old Tiger...

Marsupial, or circus animal, or dingo overgrown...

Being in it with Eddie, even with Eddie scared, was better than being alone.

"It's getting cold," Eddie said.

He was shivering, she knew. Well, she was shivering, too, not only from cold. From the thought of it all. From the long, long night stretching ahead into an unimaginable bleakness of spirit.

All those people sitting down to dinner. All those people with nice hot cups of tea. If Eddie filled his lungs. If Eddie bellowed. Who could say? Some might hear; the sound running back through the rifts and folds and gullies of the land as the sounds of the coach had come the other way. But Eddie didn't want them to know.

Eddie keeping his voice down whenever he spoke. Eddie very jumpy about the bad men in the old mine-workings and caves, perhaps not far below. And that old Tiger. And the ghosts; the boys who died thirty years ago; and the men who died for gold; terrified ghosts; raging ghosts.

"Shelter," he said. "We'll break down leafy branches." But his voice was thick and slow and he made no move.

He was taking shallow breaths through his mouth, quickly.

"And make a mia-mia," Rachel said.

"I suppose."

All over the world all those people sitting down to supper, as if they hadn't had enough when they'd had their dinners. And getting into nice cosy beds with hot bricks wrapped in flannel. Draught-stoppers up to the doors. Windows shut. Stoves still warm. Night-lights on shelves. Cooking smells still through the houses. Smells like Cornish pasties. Auntie Lizzie with something special always for Fridays.

If it's Cornish pasties, Rachel thought, and I'm not there, I'll die.

Rachel and Eddie, waiting to start freezing.

People coming, perhaps, late into the night. Coming with hurricane lamps and stern grey faces.

Eddie shivered audibly. "It's cold. . . We'll be carried away with icicles breaking off. They'll be roaring at us, shouting at us. . . I don't know. What are we doing here? You watch 'em. They'll bring the stocks back in. All the Hobsons and Herberts chucking rotten eggs at us. In disgrace. You in disgrace because of me."

"If we run on the spot," Rachel said, "we won't get frozen."

Eddie sighed. "Run on the spot and we won't get frozen."

Could you run on the spot for hours and hours and hours?

In disgrace, Eddie said. To that Councillor Hobson might add, "Is this the sort of family you want in the place of honour round here? Instead of me. Your stalwart and champion these many years. His eldest daughter. Church organist, they say. Out in the bush all night with a boy. Vote for me. Vote for Dave Hobson. For dignity and propriety."

Dad losing the election because of her.

"This shelter," Eddie said. "We've got to make it." His voice was still so slow, his breathing so shallow and fast. And like her he was shivering from more than the cold. She knew.

The fall of the big hero, but that wasn't fair. He was still there. His height. His presence. His strength. But he was only a boy, and scared. And shy. And ashamed. And at a loss.

All this she felt. All this she knew. She wanted to say, "Oh, Eddie. Don't worry. I don't mind if you're scared, though I wish you weren't. Do you think we're going to get out of here? Safe and sound? Or do you reckon they'll find us later on? Too much later on? Because I mean why? Why would they ever look here? Do you think we'll just go, just disappear, like those boys? What made me come through that silly fence? What made me act so mad? I know you'd never have hurt me in a lifetime, but how was I to know it was you?"

Aloud she said nothing.

Side by side. The cold settling. Like before, cold was getting into her brain.

Must have been in his brain, too. The cold. Or was it just everything, everything, looming like something much too high to climb?

CHAPTER SEVEN

Evermore Hellebore

A change came.

Slowly, almost silently, the change became an awareness that in turn became a sound.

Rachel was about to say, "Something's moving in the ground."

She heard Eddie's breath catch and felt the closure of his fingers on one arm. Then on the other. Felt his fingers tightening as if he had a dozen or more to spare.

She'd heard girls say that boys had as many arms as octopuses and as many fingers as the leaves of trees.

She felt herself being drawn to him as if he needed contact, or strength, or nerve, and intended to get it from her.

It hurt. She wished he'd let go.

"They're coming," he said.

His voice was low. Barely above a whisper.

Rachel was frightened. Unnerved.

"They're out already," he said. "They're coming. The blighters. They haven't given me a chance to get out on my own."

He was holding on so tightly, taking out of her all her strength, all her nerve.

Let go, Eddie. Please. My arm. It hurts. It's not a thick arm like yours.

"Do we let them know?" he said. "We can't let them find us, Rachel. Not here."

Did it matter? Did it matter any more? Apparently yes.

It was as if he was running all ways and running in all directions. Part of the change. Part of being different from before.

He was shaking with nerves.

"It's a horse," she said suddenly, desperately, trying to get things back to a level she could understand.

"I don't hear a horse."

But he was wrong.

The sound of the horse was plain.

"I hear someone calling," he said. "Calling our names. But from where? From which way? I don't know which way. I don't hear a horse. What's a horse got to do with it?"

"Out in the paddocks," she said, "like I hear you when you're riding the plough horse. The same sound."

"I don't hear it."

She wished he'd take a really deep breath, take a pause. He worried her more and more.

"I don't think they're calling," she said. "I think it's a song. Eddie! Listen!"

Clearly, a song was to be heard.

Something about gold for the poor, and hey nonny nonny, and bang bang bang.

Something about hellebore evermore.

Hellebore?

Coming in fast. Coming in from where?

That fellow was drunk. That fellow was as drunk as a lord. As drunk as Lord Bacchus, if not more.

Eddie's fingers were so tight that the bruises were forming.

"The direction," he whispered. "What direction is he? He's coming so fast."

"If he's coming through here," Rachel said, "he'll fall down a shaft. He's too drunk to know up from down."

"Don't talk so loud!"

"He can't hear. He's out in the paddocks... You know, I think it's Ole Roll."

"Ole Roll hasn't got a horse."

"He's got one now. Oh dear, if he's stolen it! A coach horse. Oh dear... I've heard him singing songs like it before..."

There'll be gold for the poor all around, we sang,
With a hey nonny nonny and a bang bang bang,
But the gold for the poor went home with the rich,
To their hey nonny nonny and their bang bang bang.

Hellebore evermore is in store for the poor,
What the hell's evermore hellebore for the poor?
With a hey nonny nonny and a bang bang bang,
For the fleas and the poor do offend us, they sang.

"It's a funny-sounding tune," Rachel said. "There's nothing like it in the hymn book."

Ole Roll went on with the next verse, the eighteenth or the nineteenth, or whatever it might have been.

"I'm glad he's got a horse," Rachel said. "I'm really glad now. That's nice. He'll be getting home out of the cold. He's much too old to be sleeping under trees."

Farther away went Ole Roll. Farther away.

Eddie's fingers were relaxing from her arms. They'd been so cruelly tight.

The relief.

"He'd have to be riding through the paddocks, wouldn't he? There isn't anywhere else. So he's shown us where the paddocks lie. For the first time in his life that old drunk's been some use."

"For the second time," Rachel said. "He saved me tonight. He could've saved us again if you'd called."

"He couldn't save a fly. He couldn't walk ten steps without falling over. But by golly I'm glad it wasn't anyone looking for us. It's a weight off my mind. What do you mean he saved you tonight? What are you on about now?"

"He laid into them with his cane."

"Laid into — them?"

"The boys. That whole mob of stupid young kids. You and your hoodlum mates were the second lot, Eddie Crawford."

Immediately she regretted it. Immediately she knew

she didn't mean it. Immediately she heard his protest and
felt it strike through her.

"*We're not hoodlums!*"

"I'm sorry. I'm sorry. I take it back. I didn't mean it."

"We're not hoodlums! I've never been a hoodlum! You
mustn't say it!"

"I won't. I won't. I won't say it again. I'm sorry. It was
a whole mob of stupid young kids whooping it up. Ole
Roll cracked their heads. He laid into them with his cane.
He took care of me."

Eddie had gone quiet again, and distant again, though
he was no more than a step away.

"Are you saying you've been chased twice tonight?"

"I think it sounds like it, don't you?"

Eddie sighed.

There were things she thought she ought to say, but she
didn't. She waited on him until she felt the cold again.
Felt it settling again. Felt the awful worry of it again.

"I don't think shelter's going to work," he said. "I think
we've got to go. We've got to try. At least we know where
the paddocks lie. Are you game? Do you mind if we try?"

"I'll do what you want to do," she said.

"And that old drunk looked after you? Really and
truly?"

"Yes."

He took her arm, her thin arm, not with the pressure
or hurt of before. "I'll look after you, too. I'll get you out
of here. I promise. I'm not a hoodlum. I wouldn't hurt a
hair of your head. I'm so sorry, Rachel. Just so sorry it's
happened. I'm never going to believe it. . . ."

She had to say it: "Getting out of here —"

"Yes?"

"It's not the way you're facing. It's round a bit. It's
round a lot. It's back there, actually."

"No," he said, as if regretting he had to disagree.

"But it is."

"It's not! It can't be! Ole Roll went through directly in front of us."

"He didn't, Eddie. He went through directly behind us!"

He sighed, and in a moment or two groaned, "Oh my gawd... Look, Rachel, my sense of direction was good enough to get me in here. I heard what I heard."

"I've been hearing lots of things from in here," she said. "Directions keep changing all the time."

"Which is what I'm saying. I know what I've heard and where I heard it. Your ears I can't vouch for."

"I'm not confident, Eddie, if you go this way."

"Well, get behind me then. One or two clear steps behind. Then when I fall over the edge into the Hot Pot you've got time to stop."

"I don't think that's fair, Eddie."

"Well, it's what you're saying! Fair or not! I *cannot* go in the opposite direction. I can't *do* that."

"Oh dear," Rachel said.

"Get behind me. It's safer for you to be there, anyway. And put your feet down good and firm. A sprained ankle would be the very last thing."

"Oh, Eddie, I'm afraid you're going to walk over the edge. I really am."

"I'll take my time. I'll be extra extra careful. Will that please you? Then if we do come to the edge you'll have the satisfaction of knowing you were right."

"I'm not worried about being right."

"I'm not worried about it either! Because you're wrong."

"Eddie, we mustn't fight."

"We're not fighting. It's what my mum and dad call a difference of opinion."

She sighed. Such a sigh. "You've no idea," she said, "how much I hope you're right. I really would like to think I was going home to my dinner. There might be

Cornish pasties at our house. What are you having at your house?"

"The whip, unless I'm dead lucky."

Eddie was moving, and she followed on, a couple of steps behind. Well, it was what he had asked her to do. Any more than a couple of steps and she might have lost him in the darkness. But she could see it happening. She could see the curve. How had he found her? A fluke, he'd called it. A fluke it had been.

"Eddie! You're heading in a curve! You must be able to see it!"

Back came his voice, with a touch of irritation. "Don't be stupid. I'm heading straight as a die."

"All right," Rachel said, "I really do hate to say this, after all the effort you've made. But if you think you've got to keep going your way, I think I'd better go mine."

"Look here!" Eddie stopped. His voice was thin, was impatient. Yes, and cross. "I'm *not* heading in a curve."

"Oh my goodness," Rachel said. "But you are. Just like drawing a circle."

"I don't believe it."

"I don't know where you're heading any more, because you're going left all the time."

"How do you think I found you? Because I couldn't hear straight or see straight or do anything straight?"

"I don't know," Rachel said. "Perhaps you weren't as tired then. Or as cross."

"Perhaps I hadn't been listening to all your yap. You do as I say. You stick behind."

He stepped off, and that was it.

He wasn't there to stick behind.

CHAPTER EIGHT

Storm of Stones

The astonishment!

It was happening.

This shocking thing was happening: quartz rubble, dark, mossy, and moist, was moving underfoot, Rachel knowing she was in the middle of it.

Oh, the realisation. The self-condemnation. The hundred warnings. The thousand warnings. Ignored.

From the day the language began to make sense, from the day you could decide for yourself to go where you pleased, they'd told you: "Keep out of there."

And long ago they'd put the fence across. And a short while ago she'd thrust through.

In the instant that the movement began she could see herself lying dead, and she felt the hurt and the pain of it, and the loss of everyone at home, and the loss of all the unlived years. All those years gone in an instant, never to be.

She said goodbye, said I'm sorry, I really did listen, I really did understand, yet here I am, here I go.

Backwards was the only way, hands thrown up as if to ward it off, as if to live a second longer, reeling back from the brink of the widening abyss.

There was a hole in the earth and she saw the depth of it, the darkness of it, the breadth of it.

There wasn't any need to see it with your eyes to be visually aware.

Almost in the same instant, backwards ended suddenly like a wall or a hedge.

The shock of that, too.

The outer branches of a tree, branches in all directions, low to the ground, from a broad, dense wattle with a heavy smell and sharpness and brittleness and stickiness. Also in an instant she felt as if a door had shut her off from the old world where she used to be.

An enormity. An unbelievable thing.

She fought physically against it, went lunging frantically in every direction except ahead, but no way yielded more than briefly.

A flash through her mind: she thought of the dog on the chain.

Oh, the explosion of feelings and thoughts and realisations.

Oh, for the world to stand still, to become quiet again, to become solid again, where life happened at a pace you could bear.

"There's no way back."

Perhaps she cried her fear aloud. Perhaps everything happened so quickly there wasn't a word. Perhaps in a moment the mouth of the Earth must open for Rachel as it had opened for Eddie and take her away.

As quickly as Eddie she'd go, as awfully, and no one would know when or where or how. For who would look here, after having warned her a thousand times? Or was she already gone as Eddie had gone, once the only unordinary boy in town? Was this what came after the familiar world was lost?

"Where's Rachel?" they'll say in the old world back there. And they'll answer, "She disappeared on the way home."

"Where's Eddie?" they'll say. "Has he run off with Rachel? Incredible. A nice boy like him and a nice girl like her?"

Eddie'd gone down, Rachel knew.

Eddie with the mullock all around. Yellow mud. Grey mud. Rotten timbers. Eddie in the middle as if caught in a flood rushing away.

On Friday Eddie went to school but on Monday he won't be there. Next year, Continuation School, and then the world. Eddie would have made his mark out there.

Rachel, on Monday, won't be at school either.

People will say, "Would they really run away? They've never been together on their own. She's not fourteen."

Was it seconds that it lasted, this slipping and sliding of earth? Or were there minutes of it like a gruelling pain? Was it happening still? Rachel would never know until she quietened the roarings in her head, the noises she threw up like barriers inside herself to block out the noises of the stones.

She went thrusting with her arms through the tree, clutching for stronger holds, trying to claw herself up from the ground, still caught in the panic of waiting for the Earth to take her, or for all to fall quiet.

Something might have happened, or stopped happening. Something might have gone back to the way it used to be.

A kind of quiet, with rustling sounds that might have been in the tree or in the ground. Or most alarmingly in both. Everything around might still have been sliding in a block with the mullock into the great hole, carrying Rachel down.

She was afraid to breathe, but couldn't arrest her great gulps of air, though she tried so hard not to move in any way. Her throat burned and her chest heaved and there was no silencing of her moaning, no stilling of her fear, no stopping of that scented, heavy, cold air that cut into her. Her mind went one way, laying down the law; her body went another way and made different rules.

The world was still.

Perhaps.

Perhaps if she twitched a finger it would move, would roar again, and rumble, and slip.

Over and over she told herself, "It's still. It's stopped. I'm sure."

The old world had become solid again and quiet again.

When had it ended, this storm of stones? Just now or minutes ago? Or had it been a single horrifying moment stretched out of all proportion?

Frogs were making echoes of hollowness as if they croaked within great and empty halls.

Eddie wasn't there.

Nowhere could Rachel hear Ole Roll on his borrowed or stolen steed, singing of poor man's gold.

No one was out of doors.

No one came calling for Rachel.

Eddie was gone.

What do you do about the next moment when you scarcely dare breathe your way into it because the fragile world might not stand the strain?

"Rachel. Are you there?"

The shock of hearing her name! Oh, the rushing of her pulse, the flooding up of tears.

"Rachel, are you safe?"

"You're alive," she said.

"Why cry? What about a cheer?"

Heaven only knew how long it was before she could say, "I thought you were gone."

"You're not the only one. What's happened to you?"

"I'm holding onto a tree."

At least her voice wasn't causing the world to slip again and slide and roar.

Then Eddie said, "I'm in a shaft. Or a subsidence. It's not moving any more, thank God. Have things gone quiet near you? Is it solid there?"

"I wouldn't know."

"You must know. You're standing on it, aren't you?"

"I'm keeping my feet off it. I'm keeping my weight off it."

"Well don't. Get a good hold if you feel you must, but then put your weight down."

"I don't want to."

"Be a sport, Rachel. You sound real near. If it's solid there it might be solid here. Which'll give me a better chance. I've got to get out."

"I know you have."

"Well, get a good hold and let your weight down. I daren't twitch a muscle till I know."

"What if the stones start moving again? What'll that do to you? And to me? Wouldn't it be better to stay as we are?"

"Doing what? Waiting for the stones to start moving again of their own accord? Waiting here all night maybe? Waiting till we die?"

She was afraid he was buried, but wouldn't say it, couldn't ask the question, could only stammer, "Can't you get out?"

"Right now I'm not going to try. But if I can't you'll be running for help."

"Eddie... I don't know how."

"You'll be doing it, Rachel."

He wasn't thinking past himself.

He was being selfish.

She wanted to say, "So you're scared to move. What about me? Haven't you heard a word I've said? I'm scared to move, too." But she held it back.

He said, "I'm stuck in a heap of mullock. The mullock's probably stuck in a shaft. I've got muck and stones up to my hips and I can't move. I don't reckon I could if I wanted to. I'm tryin' hard not to panic. I don't want to drop any farther. It might go down and down and down."

"And you might be on the bottom. If I start stones moving again you might get the lot on your head."

But inside she said, "I've got to do it though. I'm better off than he is. I've got to put my weight on the ground. I'll count to three or something, and then do it. It's not much he's asking."

Eddie was saying, almost as if talking to himself, "I

can't believe it. I think she's telling me I've got to stay
stuck because she's too scared to breathe."

Inside her head, Rachel said, "If I put my feet down
and the ground moves, it's all over. All over for Eddie. All
over for me."

He was saying, "Are you making out you can't hear
me? Don't you care what happens down here?"

Inside her head, Rachel said, "It's all he's asking. . .
One. Two. Three."

It was done.

Eddie was saying, "Have you fainted off in a funk
again? Are you paralysed with fear again? If you've gone
and fainted on me. . ."

Her feet were down. No weight was bearing on the
tree. All of it was on the ground.

She was shaking violently with nerves and there was an
alarming movement underfoot, though different from
before.

Eddie cried out, "Of all the people in the world to be
stuck with in a jam."

Had the movement stopped? Or was the lot about to
rush away bearing her in its midst?

Eddie was talking. Perhaps talking eased the panic.
She had no idea what he said.

"It's firm," she stammered.

"What's that?"

"The ground's *firm*!" She shouted on the last word and
Eddie came back sharply.

"Would you know?"

"I'd not be saying it was firm if it wasn't."

"Thanks for getting round to it then. If you have."

She saw red. He had no idea how hard she'd tried!

Her foot flashed out angrily and quartz stones as big as
eggs flew from the toe of her right boot.

"What'd you do that for?" Eddie howled. "You trying
to kill me of fright? You trying to start a slide? You threw
stones at me."

"Do you believe me now?"

Eddie was panting, clear to hear, but her anger had gone. She'd had her say.

She had to wait on him a surprising time, and her big toe throbbed so furiously it just had to be turning black and blue.

"Chucking those stones was silly."

"I didn't chuck them. I kicked them."

"Well, you've proved the point."

"That's what I meant to do."

"I don't want to fight any more."

"I wasn't fighting. You were calling me a liar. I was telling you I wasn't."

"Being stuck down here isn't funny."

She was about to say, "Being up here isn't funny either." But she didn't. Instead, she went on, "Now you know it's firm can you come up out?"

He sighed. "No."

"Why can't you?"

He sighed again. "I'm stuck. But I'm going to start throwing stones and I'll keep on throwin' 'em till I can get my legs out."

"You mean throwing them up out of there? From round you?"

"If you can kick them one way, I can throw them the other. Let's hope we don't start a slide. Duck your head. Here they come."

CHAPTER NINE

A Beautiful Big Toe

Rachel sat on the cold damp ground and nursed her toe, criticising it.

"I hate you," she said.

The world was full of matters much more urgent, but the only way of enduring them was to be otherwise engaged.

She concluded it was a terrible bit of bad luck being born with a big toe half as long as your foot. Well, measured in general terms.

"I don't know why I'm cursed with you," she said.

Almost every evening there it was, looking ridiculous, poking out through the latest hole in her regulation black stockings. There were Rennie and Rose always tripping over this or that. Everyone stumbling about the house, except Dad and Auntie Lizzie, which meant it came from Mother's side of the family.

Poor Mother, unable to defend the honour of her name.

"It's the fault of the Halls," Auntie Lizzie said. "It's a well-known Cornish institution. Got from scratching in the dirt like puppy dogs over a couple of thousand years looking for tin."

Rachel sitting on the cold damp ground trying to ignore the perilous world while Eddie's stones came thudding down to remind her of it.

"What about you, Rachel?" Eddie called.

"All right," she mumbled in a shiver.

Poor Eddie throwing stones.

Not thinking about him caught in that hole up to his

middle was the only way Rachel could stand it. Every time it touched her mind it touched a panic; Eddie clawing at stones, heaving them away, some running back rustling like reeds. Very ominous. Then crashing down all around, glancing off the tree, crashing through vegetation, crashing on other stones. Sparks striking. Chips flying.

Trying not to yelp when bits hit her. Trying not to notice. Trying not to shout at him when a stone as big as a cricket ball struck her hip. He'd never mean to hurt her. She knew about Eddie.

Rachel came first with Eddie except at mealtimes and in the cricket season. Which Rachel felt was reasonable in part because nothing should interfere with meals. Cricket was another matter.

Rachel knew because Chrissie told her.

What were best friends for? If not to share secrets?

"My brother," Chrissie said, a year or two back, "is getting sweet on you. Had you noticed?"

Nothing of the kind had ever crossed her mind.

"Take a look at him in church, why don't you?" Chrissie said.

So she looked up from the organ in the middle of a hymn and two soulful eyes were looking back. Looked as though he had a terrible sickness. It caused her, immediately, to forget her place, bringing from Auntie Lizzie a sharp glance over the top of her hymn book and an expression of surprise from Dad that his brilliant daughter could miss a bar and a half.

"What about you up there, Rachel," Eddie called. "Are you still all right?"

Well, she was and she wasn't. "Mumble, mumble," she said, shivering, wanting to be far, far away.

Eddie went on throwing stones.

Crashing, chipping, sparking. Sounds on two levels. The other was a much quieter sound, that ominous rustling, so sinister. Stones running back.

Trying hard, hard, not to think of Eddie below the ground, as if his funeral with the white ostrich plumes was only a matter of time.

The fear was hurting her.

Perhaps there was a similarity to the long hours of the middle of the night, when there were noises and movements and endless anxieties and no sleep to take you away to safety; trying to spell difficult words, trying to count up to ten thousand, trying to recite cities of the British Empire:

> London, Hong Kong, Kingston, Leeds,
> England sows the far-flung seeds,
> Cape Town, Georgetown, Singapore,
> Winnipeg to sunny shore,
> Cardiff, Christchurch, Rangoon, Perth,
> How they reach across the Earth,
> Dublin, Delhi and Dundee,
> Why have they done this to me?
>
> Far-flung cities get my goat,
> One and all they stick my throat,
> Who gave the Englishman a boat?
>
> Preacher says God's will was done,
> Teacher says salute the gun,
> On the Empire sets no sun.

"*Rachel!*"

"Yes."

"You didn't answer!"

"I didn't hear."

"I thought I'd knocked you out."

"I'm still here. And I'm glad you're still there... I mean, I don't mean —"

"I *know* what you mean. And I want you to get this stuck in your bean."

But he fell silent.

She said, "I'm listening."

Eventually, as if breathless, he went on, "If I don't start a slide I should be getting my legs free. If the stones slip... If they do, you're not to move. You're to stay where you are."

"Are you ordering me?"

"Hang on to your tree till the people come. They'll be out soon. Coming from all directions. Dogs. Lights. Heaven knows what. Call them in. Let them find you. Don't go looking for them. Do you promise?"

"Why would they come here, unless one of your mates tells them? I can't see that happening. Do you really reckon anyone would come in here after dark?"

"Our dads would. Maybe no one else, but they would. I'm talking about your life, Rachel. It depends on staying where you are."

"You were only just saying that I'd have to run for help."

"I've changed my mind."

"What if you change it again and say Rachel do this, Rachel do that?"

"I won't, but if I do, take no notice. If we both end up a long way down, we're dead. While you're hanging on to that tree you've got a hope of getting out of here, and so have I. It's my life, too. Have you got that stuck in your bean?"

"I heard you, if that's what you mean."

"I mean more than that." He went shrill. "You mustn't leave that tree, no matter what. We need someone able to yell. Someone able to direct people in. Someone able to see what's going on. There's no one but you. It depends on you. Promise."

"I'm not crossing my heart to anything."

She felt about it so strongly she surprised herself. Was that Rachel talking? Old scaredy-cat Rachel?

"If anything goes wrong, Eddie Crawford, we'll see what happens then. You get on with it."

He went quiet, as before, and seemed to become a centre of quietness that spread. Rachel began to feel it, almost like deep water.

Eddie said, "All right. I'm getting on with it. I'll try."

Immediately the quietness returned and Rachel became intensely cold, as if a sickness had come upon her, for in her mind, suddenly, she saw Eddie fall amid a roar of collapse. Or was it that he sank as if stones had turned to treacle? Was he suffocated, or lifeless, life snuffed out or crushed out somewhere below?

"Rachel."

"Yes."

Her voice must have been difficult to recognise.

"I've got my legs out. I really, really have. Throwing out those stones. That's what did it. . . ."

My beautiful big toe, Rachel thought, that's what gave him the idea. Who cares if it hurts for a week. My big toe has got Eddie out of there.

She thought then she could see his hand reaching up like the hand of a drowning person.

"All I've got to do now," he said, "is get myself out." He was markedly short of wind. "There's a branch of a tree. Is it yours? I see it against the sky."

That's strange, she thought. There isn't a hand. I wonder if there ever was?

"Did you hear me, Rachel?"

"Yes."

"The branch!"

"What about it?"

"Move it. Move it. I want to know if it's the right one."

"The right one for what?"

"To get a hold of. To drag myself up."

"How far down are you then?"

"Not far."

Something was going on.

Had the collapsing roar been real? How far down was he, really and truly?

"How far's not far?" she said.

"Far enough."

What was Eddie up to? She felt a new uneasiness. Was he asking her to move, to go against the promise he'd tried to exact from her?

"What branch are you talking about?"

"You must be able to see it. It's long and low. It's there. Right there."

He sounded a bit hysterical. On a real edge. The edge of pain perhaps.

The branch was off to her left. There was no other. A long branch, low, but not where she'd imagined Eddie to be. A distinct distance to the left. She'd not seen the hand.

"The branch!"

"Yes," she said.

"Move it. Move it, will you!"

"I have to get to it first."

"Oh."

There was dismay in Eddie's voice. A new breathlessness.

Yes, Rachel told herself. He's still stuck! Throwing out the stones didn't work.

Then she asked of herself, "How do I reach the branch without letting go?"

Her fingers were separating, were extending, were stretching. They were answering the question for her and she had to go with them towards the branch, the only branch there was, far out of reach.

The alarming insecurity, the fright of knowing that her support, her safety, had gone, the stretching in vain, the overbalancing into three rapid frightened steps, a cry, and she thudded into the branch, hung on, clung on, swaying on the spring of it, sideways, and up and down.

"That's it! That's it!"

It might have been right for Eddie, but her heartbeat was going crazy. She felt light-headed and dizzy and sick, as if she had farther yet to fall.

"That's it, Rachel. Bend it. Push it down. Farther than that."

Getting her wind back. Getting her strength back. Getting her nerve.

"Bring it down, Rachel. More."

"In a minute. In a minute."

Was there really a hand this time, reaching up from the darkness underground? Or was it still in the mind?

"Oh, make it now, Rachel. Please."

Impulsively and alarmingly, she bounced on the branch.

"I can't reach," he said.

Not a cry. Just a tired statement.

She couldn't believe it.

There was such finality in his voice, yet at the bottom of the bounce the tip of the branch must have gone below ground level.

That meant there hadn't been a hand at any time.

She was ready to be sick. The sickness was there, waiting, forcing her to swallow.

The sweet scent of the tree was overpowering.

This wattle, she thought. They're all the same. Any bit of wind can bring them down. They're so brittle. They snap. What am I doing to myself, bouncing on this thing? He was right when he said I wasn't to move. We're doing what he said we weren't to do.

"It's too high. It's too high. It's not fair."

Eddie was talking again, voice at the edge of hysteria again, breaking his own rule again, asking more of her, more all the time.

Mightn't have been fair for him. Wasn't fair for her either.

It made her guilty, made her cross. Never in her life, knowing what she was doing, had she wilfully risked her life.

"Life's from God," Dad said. "A gift beyond understanding. To be cherished and defended. Never to be disgraced or treated with disrespect or thrown away. Remember that."

"It's too high for me," Eddie said.

Dad smashed into and smashed out of a blazing house with a child in his arms on the day all the kids from Donkey Gully had tea and sandwiches in Carter Hooke's front parlour because it was not safe to go home. The afternoon that saw much of Donkey Gully burn, and crippled Terry Herbert, four years old, all but perish in terror in a locked house.

Whose life counted for more? The one risked or the one saved?

"Rachel!"

No one gave Dad a medal. No one knew the "authorities" had to be advised, not even Carter Hooke or Doctor Savage. Perhaps they thought medals fell from Heaven, from the hand of the All-Knowing.

Dad got burns and a huge hug from Terry.

Rachel cried out in despair and leant on the branch, leant forward with numbness, and inched farther forward until the branch was bending most desperately and swaying and jolting and tugging at the length of her body, stretching her almost to snapping point, and she didn't know how to get back or by what madness she had allowed herself into such a wildly unstable position, for she was so far forward her head was lower than her feet, and her school satchel had fallen about her face, and her spine was arched painfully, and the toes of her boots barely touched the ground.

"Back! Back!"

It was Eddie, Eddie's voice, Eddie's head in her face.

"I can't get back."

An elbow jammed into her collar bone.

"Push. Get back."

Everything was swaying and creaking and jolting and she was exhausted and soaked in sweat.

"*Push.*"

There was no strength in her back, but were her feet on the ground? Was she pushing? Was the arch in her spine becoming less stressed? Was she inching back as she had inched forward, really, truly, every movement taking all the strength she could find, and all the nerve?

She was sitting in the midst of stripped foliage and winter blossom and broken twigs and jagged ends.

Eddie, like some kind of giant spider, was for a moment visible crawling by.

Nothing was said.

In a while she mastered herself and was able to breathe without noisy labour. Then she heard Eddie crying.

"Rachel," she said to herself, "you mustn't ever tell, not even Chrissie."

CHAPTER TEN

Paid in Full

Eddie's fingers closed on her arm. "Come away from here. Enough of here..."

She was drawn a few steps by the pressure of his hand.

He'd broken a length from the tree and stripped it of foliage and used it like a blind man's cane, feeling ahead, poking at the ground.

"I can see a bit," he said. "It must be the moon."

She continued to move with the leading pressure of his hand, but wasn't seeing much, certainly not the moon. It was like making your way through the dark parts of a dream.

"Should've thought of a stick before," he said, "but you don't, do you, until afterwards? You got me out of there. You know that, Rachel?"

"Yes."

"I'd never have got anywhere if you hadn't pushed the branch down."

"I know."

"No way of working myself free even. Stones kept rolling back." His voice went hoarse.

"Why say anything, Eddie? Let it go."

Rachel felt wise; felt that having been through it was enough. There were feelings for which words were not needed or were too much.

"We've really got to get out of here," he said.

"I think so."

"Staying here all night? We can't do it, Rachel. Waiting for them to come? No. I don't know what they'll do to you, but they'll flay me alive."

He went on poking the ground and taking her ahead a step at a time.

"I'm seeing a bit," he said. "Perhaps your eyes get used to it."

She knew his eyes hadn't got used to it; she knew he wasn't seeing anything except dark and shapeless masses; but terrible events had to reach a point of saturation beyond which nothing more could happen. You'd have to start laughing. If the ground opened up again you'd go down laughing. You had nothing left to be scared with. Your innards had been twisted dry like an old towel.

"I think we're getting somewhere," Eddie said.

What was she to say? It didn't look different to her. Nothing but night. Nothing but bush. Nothing but the dull, cold, and treacherous presence underfoot of mullock and stones.

I want my dinner now, she thought, and then bed. Beautiful bed. All nice and warm and soft and safe, sinking off to sleep, with Dad and Auntie Lizzie in the next room playing cribbage.

"Fifteen two, fifteen four, fifteen six, and a pair makes eight."

One of these days she might understand that language. But now the sound of it would be enough in those hollow chambers close to sleep; the voices coming through the wall so loudly you'd think there was an empty place inside your head, a room with a high ceiling, for voices to echo in. Not that she'd be telling anyone, or there'd be rude comments from Rennie and Rose. *Rachel's got a hole in her head, a hole in her head . . .*

Staying in front of the younger ones; you had to, you know. Eddie and Chrissie wouldn't know anything about that. Everyone at their house expected them to mess up simple tasks, to say idiotic things. Hardly a year apart, Eddie and Chrissie, the youngest of a large family of patronising elders who were still surprised to find Eddie and Chrissie out of their romper suits.

Eddie was out of his. There couldn't be any doubt of it now. Eddie with his fingers tighter on her arm than they needed to be. He wasn't being familiar though. Not like that strange Eddie lying in wait with his mates.

Eddie Crawford in wait for Rachel.

Oh, Eddie.

Believing that story of his. Waiting to walk her home? Would she ever be able, really, to believe it? Eddie excited from his fight with Willie Herbert in the battle paddock. Getting carried away. The same as the young kids chasing her along the high street. Excited in the same way. For the same reason. From the fight. From being in it. Eddie Crawford flattening Willie Herbert's nose.

She was aware of Eddie's fingers on her arm, guiding her, drawing her along, even hurting her.

Eddie had come in here for her when the others had run away. Eddie had almost died trying to get her out. But there wasn't a debt. She wasn't saying thank you. She'd paid in full.

Eddie and Rachel, they were even.

He'd come to a halt. She wasn't sure when.

He said, "We should be out of here, by now. We've come a lot farther than I ever did finding you."

His voice was thin. She knew the sound of it from before, and knew the signs. Eddie was beginning to frazzle.

"I'm not sure any more," he said. "Am I going in circles again?"

"I've not been trying to see."

"But I'm watching a star," he said, as if bewildered. "Going as straight as a die towards a star."

"You mean straight up into the air?"

Oh, it was a feeble joke, and it failed to amuse him, and when she wearily thought of it, it didn't amuse her either.

"All stars look the same to me, Eddie," she said, but she was almost too tired to give an opinion, or to stand there, or to support him...

All at once she became aware of it! He was leaning on her. She was holding him up!

"Are you sick or something?" she said unexpectedly and with indignation. "Stand on your own feet."

She could feel the rise and fall of his breath and the easing away of his weight almost at the instant that he hissed, "Did you hear that?"

She did. Indeed she did. Her own name trumpeted across the countryside. Unmistakably Auntie Lizzie's call from a direction that seemed to be directly *there*.

"She's coming along the creek!"

A new purpose was in Eddie's voice and in the grip of his hand. "We weren't far enough around. We were going parallel to the fence."

"Oh, careful," she cried.

"I'm being careful."

He was jabbing at the ground and shuffling ahead, stumbling ahead, dragging her, muttering man-sized words that didn't go all that well with Eddie. It was strange to hear him so desperate, so grown up, as if he had to use strong words or turn back into a boy again.

"Come on, come on," he urged, as if he had a whip to a dawdling beast. "Move yourself, Rachel."

She tried.

Suddenly, they were upon it, the old post-and-rail fence.

They were there.

"Oh, thank you," Eddie cried.

He hurled the stick into the open, into the heights, as if to bring down the stars.

"We've done it!"

Eddie tumbled over the top rail; Rachel thrust between them; both came up scrambling, running.

"We're out!"

The new effort dragged from Rachel more than she knew she had to give, somehow running, somehow keeping up, somehow doing as Eddie demanded.

"We're out!"

They were in the paddocks, the wide, wide open paddocks. There were the forest fringes. There were the thousands of stars clear to see from open ground. There was the open run home. You could *see* it.

Oh, her big toe and her tiredness. Tiredness like a sickness, the way Eddie was sick with tiredness.

Amazing, that you could move. A miracle. It was like being raised from a sickbed to run in a race.

She cried suddenly, "My satchel."

She dug in her heels in panic, dug in her toes, almost wrenched him from his feet.

"My satchel's gone."

"Too bad. Too bad."

"I've got to go back for it. My satchel."

"You can't go back."

"It's in the hole. I remember when it fell. And then I forgot."

"We're not going back!"

"My music. My homework. My things. My satchel."

He was dragging on her with a desperation almost past believing, far beyond the level she could resist or fight.

He dragged her on and on, away from the awful bushlands, away from the fence, into the open.

Auntie Lizzie's call was clear. Again it came like a trumpet. "Answer me, Rachel."

Was there anyone round about who didn't hear? Through walls and doors and windows?

The Crawfords? They must've heard. Eddie's dad. There he'd be. On his way.

"The satchel's got my name on it. They'll know. Everything has my name on it. They'll know where we've been."

There were the lights of the Crawford house. Lit up as if to light the way home for the errant boy — doing what out there in the dark? They'd be bound to ask. A light was moving near the house. That'd be the real end; Auntie Lizzie and Eddie's dad coming together.

There was Auntie Lizzie's light, farther along, beside

the creek. But not much farther. Auntie Lizzie calling
with a voice of astonishing penetration.

"Answer me, Rachel!"

"Don't tell," Eddie cried. Or groaned. Or moaned.
"Oh, please, Rachel. I'd never tell on you, no matter
what."

All those grown-up bits, the desperate grown-up bits,
had gone. He was bent double, as if vomiting.

"I'll never live it down if you tell. They'll never understand."

"Eddie! Eddie! I'm waiting on you, Eddie!"

No mistake about that voice. There was only one man
it could be.

Eddie had gone, stumbling towards the lights of the
Crawford house, towards the light that must have been
held by his dad, towards whatever the retribution was
going to be. Rachel could see him for a few seconds only,
then couldn't see him. Perhaps he'd fallen. Perhaps he'd
headed another way.

Don't tell, Eddie said.

When they found the satchel, what did telling or not
telling have to do with it? She wouldn't need to tell. The
satchel would say everything and everyone would know.

The dismay that Eddie had gone.

The defencelessness of it.

"Rachel! Rachel! Rachel!"

Rachel's lungs filled, and she shrilled, "I'm coming,
Auntie Lizzie. Here I am, Auntie Lizzie."

Just to answer the call seemed like an admission of
guilt, seemed like saying, "Here I am. I've done
something terrible. Please don't notice how wicked I am.
Please take me home."

She headed for Auntie Lizzie's light, but it made no
move in her direction, just went on moving towards the
Crawford house, as if Rachel had not called at all. Eddie
would stumble into it. There he'd be; caught between
Auntie Lizzie and his dad.

I can't stand any more, Rachel thought. I can hear them all the time, but no one ever hears me. I yell. I yell and I yell and they don't hear me.

"Listen to me. Listen to me. It's me. It's Rachel."

She shrilled it, she shrieked it, until it ended in a fit of coughing, out of energy, out of breath.

"Did I hear you, Rachel? Where are you? For Heaven's sake what are you doing out here?"

Oh dear. Oh dear. She got the breath from somewhere and cried again, "I'm coming, I'm coming."

"I hope you are!"

Drawing closer on that hillside; Auntie Lizzie approaching like a storm. You could feel the change in the air. You could feel the approaching presence. No welcoming arms tonight.

Rachel trying to pull herself together, trying to think of some way of telling the truth, of making it right, without having to use Eddie's name.

But how could you think straight? You couldn't. You couldn't.

Auntie Lizzie: "Out of my mind with worry, child. What have you been doing? Where have you been? Were you in town watching that fight?"

My goodness. My goodness. She knew about Eddie; knew about Willie. News travelled faster than flying feet!

Auntie Lizzie bustling with short steps, not a hand free to lift her skirts, hurricane lamp swinging, glass part-blackened with smoke, gun tucked under her other arm, barrel catching the lamplight, words pouring up the hill in advance of her. (Please, God, while poor Eddie gets away. Don't let them meet on the hill. Don't let them crash into each other. Or we'll never explain.)

"Heavens, child, what hour do you call this to come home?"

There was nothing to say. Nothing was going to put things right. It was all decided. Everyone already knew. Auntie Lizzie wasn't a refuge tonight.

There was such a fatigue, such a fuzziness, such a fool-
ishness in Rachel, as if she should give up and fall to the
ground, or die, or scream, or beat her fists into the cold,
dew-soaked grass.

"What's the gun for, Auntie Lizzie? Are you going to
shoot me?"

"You absurd little girl."

Rachel was on the way home again, stumbling a step or
two behind, in a fog of despair, so tired and bewildered,
wanting only to cry out, "It's not fair. You don't know
anything about it. You don't know what I've been
through. You ought to know I wouldn't be watching a
fight. You're not fair."

"Are you aware of the hour, child? Are you able yet
to pick the difference between day and night? When the
sun goes down the day is done and children are at home.
That's the rule."

Auntie Lizzie's notion of what the world could do to a
kid was a million years away. Things must have been different, somehow, when she was a girl, even though they
were supposed to have been the bad days. Surely she had
to know that things could go wrong and a kid could end
up in trouble through no fault of her own? But she didn't.
And she didn't want to know.

The kids said that when ladies got to forty or fifty
they started turning crotchety and impatient and didn't
seem to care so much any more. And that when you
turned thirteen they turned against you. Never believing
you like they used to. Always accusing you of being up to
this and that when you hadn't been at all.

It hadn't happened to Rachel before.

What a time for it to start.

"Willie Herbert's nose," Rachel shrilled at Auntie
Lizzie's back. "You ask Miss Herbert. She'll tell you
I wasn't at any fight. If she remembers. Stupid Miss
Herbert. I hate her."

Auntie Lizzie looked back sharply. The lamp swung
and smoked.

"You'll not speak of your teacher like that!"

"She kept me there till all hours. What are you blaming me for? You've got to start teaching me at home. I'm sick of running wild in the dark. Everybody going inside and shutting their doors on me. I'm sick of yelling for people who don't hear and won't hear. No one caring I was lost."

"That's the last straw, Rachel Lefevre. What rubbish you speak. You've come this way every schoolday for going on eight years. You couldn't lose your way blindfolded."

CHAPTER ELEVEN

Every Man is a Mountain

Rachel somehow keeping up, somehow stumbling along behind, but no satchel thudding against her back. A back that felt exposed to all sorts of dangers, as if it should have worn a shield instead of that invisible white placard with red letters on it:

> *It's dark. I'm late. I'm wicked.*
> *I've lost my satchel.*
> *Punish me.*

Along the bank of the creek Auntie Lizzie striding, lamp in hand (lamp smoking), gun at the slope over the other shoulder, thrusting each foot hard down, each step separate, deliberate, and ominous, like the thunder of the storm.

Hair on end — Auntie Lizzie. Most remarkable. In a bun and pinned down like a coil of rope, but still managing to stand on end round the edges, as if electrified. You could practically see the glow in the dark.

Lordy, that lady was in a state.

Tonight it would have been so good for Rachel to have warm arms hugging her close.

"All's well, Rachel."

Not this time, though. This time Auntie Lizzie was giving a new performance, a continuing anger, of wanting to hear nothing or know nothing or consider nothing that failed to make her angrier.

Perhaps it was the first real rage Auntie Lizzie had ever had. Perhaps she was enjoying herself. Perhaps she'd be in a rage for the rest of her life.

"Your father," she said in a voice like the winds of winter, "will be furious."

That'd make everything marvellous. Perhaps getting in a rage was going to be a new kind of family entertainment. Next it'd be Rennie and Rose putting in their spokes. Everyone jumping up and down, shouting and screaming. They'd become the same as a lot of other houses round about. Every time you passed this house or that house there they'd be, shouting and screaming, jumping up and down, throwing things at each other. If they didn't have a fight going every few hours people round about started thinking they were away from home.

Rachel bringing up the rear, tripping and stumbling, scurrying a few steps to catch up, gulping for breath all the while, suddenly crying out, "It's not fair if Dad gets furious. He's got no right to get furious. I had to go through it all. He's only got to hear about it. And you won't bother even to do that. I think some other lady's wearing my Auntie Lizzie's clothes and she should've stayed in her own backyard where she can jump up and down and scream and shout."

"Enough! That's the last time you'll talk to me like that."

"It's the way you're talking to me."

"Enough, I said!"

Across the bridge that Dad built strode Auntie Lizzie, heels clattering. How they clattered.

Oh, what a way to end a day.

"Please God up in Heaven, this is Rachel, the one who plays the hymns on Sundays. What are you letting this happen for?"

"Poor Rennie and poor Rose!"

Upon what obscure matter was Auntie Lizzie pronouncing now?

"What about poor Rennie and poor Rose?" Rachel cried. "What's poor about them, safe and sound at home?"

"None of your doing if they *are* safe and sound. Helpless children left to fend for themselves. A world full of villainy and a cowardly terrier that couldn't save them from a mouse. And your father late beyond belief."

"What about poor me left to fend for myself? What about poor helpless Rachel? No cowardly terrier. No father either. No nothin'."

"You'll hold your tongue, Rachel. You've done your dash, my girl. Twelve years old and roving the countryside in the dark; worrying me out of my mind."

"Thirteen!"

"The older you are the worse it is, you hoyden."

"What's a hoyden?"

"Never you mind."

"I'll look it up in the dictionary!"

"You'll regret it if you do. And what about Eddie? Where does he fit in? Why were the Crawfords calling for Eddie while I was calling for you?"

"You'll have to ask the Crawfords, won't you?"

Up the path strode Auntie Lizzie, past the duck pen and the pigsty and the turkey yard and the little house and the woodheap; ducks complaining, sow protesting, gobblers gobbling.

"Rachel, pick up a log."

Past the chook-house and Mrs MacArthur and the dairy, where Auntie Lizzie briskly hung the lamp on the post (still smoking, about to smoke itself out); hens chattering, cockerel crowing, Mrs MacArthur baaing, cow kicking the wall as if to say, "What's the rumpus? What's the riot? You'll send my milk bad."

"Rachel, you're dragging your heels. Drop the wood there. In you go. Straight to the bedroom. Undress. Straight to bed."

Past the parrot cage. Parrot squawking, "Hello. Goodbye."

"*What?*" Rachel wailed. "*To bed without my tea?*"

"What! What! You'll not use the word when addressing your elders, as you've been told before."

Into the kitchen Rachel stumbled, past the covered canary cage, into the blanket of warmth and light, into the smell of Cornish pasties, so pervading it all but laid her out. Into the steam of the kettle and the tang of wood smoke and the company of Rennie and Rose, each aghast, each visibly becoming smaller as if committed to the act of vanishing from sight.

"Frank! Are you there, Frank? Is that man still not home? I've about had enough of this family for one night. Don't stand there, Rachel. To bed. Through you go."

"You can't *mean* it, Auntie Lizzie."

"I don't know why not."

Rennie and Rose and the cowardly terrier barely visible in the presence of this formidable lady, in the presence of this unspeakable crime whatever it might have been, in the presence of the malefactor, who protested, "Oh my goodness. Not without my tea. I'll die without my tea. I'd have died an hour ago except for thinking about my tea."

"Everything to be said, Rachel, has been said. To bed!"

"What've I done that's bad? You tell me. Only running like wild. Only calling here I am, here I am, no one coming to me. Only falling over. Only not able to find my way. Not even my dad coming to me."

"Be quiet and get to bed. The filth of you, as well as everything else. The state of your clothing. There's blood . . ."

"I didn't know," Rachel wailed.

"Oh dear God . . ."

Clatter went the gun across the kitchen table. Onto the floor bowled bright-red apples and one white plate. Across the floor bowled the plate on edge, out through the door, down the step, past the parrot cage, away into the night.

"Rachel. . . You've been bleeding . . ."

"I'm not," she shrieked. "I didn't. I couldn't. I don't."

Out came Auntie Lizzie's arms, wide, so wide, as if to drag Rachel in, as if to crush her to death.

"You poor child. Oh, my poor dear Rachel. I've wronged you. How could I? Who's responsible for this?"

By golly, Rachel thought, from the depths of Auntie Lizzie's bosom. The weather's changed!

"Oh, my poor dear child, who's done it? Tell me, and I'll kill him."

Rachel struggled up and out for light and air, as if Auntie Lizzie had now become a pond in which she was about to drown. Auntie Lizzie was saying, "I must know what's happened. I must be told. Rennie! Rose! You two will take yourselves up to the front parlour at once and shut the door."

"Nothing's happened, Auntie Lizzie," Rachel cried. "Just that I was scared. Just that I was frightened."

"You can't expect me to believe that. You mustn't shield people. Rennie and Rose! Why are you still here? I said to the front room."

"It's dark up there, Auntie Lizzie," Rennie wailed.

"Continue please, Rachel."

"It's only like I said, Auntie Lizzie. I couldn't see. I didn't know which way to go. And I was cold. And I lost my way. I ran into fences and bit my tongue. I fell in the prickles and bashed into trees."

"I do find it odd," Auntie Lizzie said. "I really do. Rennie and Rose, I see you haven't moved! Do I move you myself? Rachel, continue please."

Continue where? Rachel thought. Oh dear, oh dear. Auntie Lizzie being nice is almost worse than Auntie Lizzie being mad. Oh, wouldn't it be good if I could fall on the floor in a dead faint.

"It was Willie Herbert's nose, Auntie Lizzie," she cried. "It was the fight you've heard about. But I didn't see it. I wasn't there. I was having my music lesson and Miss Herbert went out of the room and didn't come back. She didn't tell me to go. She told me to wait. And she made me late. And that gang of boys was chasing me to pop me in their pot, fire going and all."

"What boys? What boys are these?"

"Ole Roll saving me —"

"Ole Roll? What are you doing with him?"

"Ole Roll saving me from their spears. Swish, swish, hitting them with his cane."

"I'll be blessed. It's gone to the poor child's head."

"Nothing's gone to my head. It's the way it was. And I was all alone. You didn't have to run halfway to Kingdom Come to get home when you were thirteen. You only had to walk into the next room. It might have been the bad days but they weren't all bad for you. And I called for help and no one heard. And I told you. I told you before. It was dark, dark, dark. And I don't want to go to awful Miss Herbert's any more, and I don't want to go to bed without my tea. I've always had my tea, every night, except I've been sick and couldn't keep it down. Not to bed without my lovely Cornish pasty. I'll die."

"For pity's sake, child, no one's going to deny you your tea, least of all me. Have you ever been sent to bed without it? Sent to bed — but never without your tea! Why isn't your father home? Why is this left to me? If he's out canvassing votes, I'll choke him. I will. I will. *Rennie!*"

Rennie jumped clear off the floor.

"Oh yes, Auntie Lizzie. I'm going, I really am."

"*Stay — if you please!* Get the bathtub down from the hook, Rennie, and put hot water in it! This week. Not next week. Now. Do you hear? Is it clear? Don't spill it. Don't scald yourself. Don't burn yourself on the stove. See if you can manage without falling flat on your face."

"Oh yes, Auntie Lizzie. I mean no, Auntie Lizzie. I mean yes, Auntie Lizzie."

"A nice soft flannel and the lavender soap please, and Rachel's hairbrush. Did you hear me, Rennie, at any stage? Get on with it then! Rose!"

Rose stammered, "I'm being very very good, Auntie Lizzie."

"You'll bring Rachel's flannel nightdress and her blue cardigan. Then you'll light the bedroom lamp and not scorch your fingers and not set fire to the house. A most important condition because your father hasn't been into Ballarat to pay the insurance. And you won't knock the lamp over when you put the glass back on and spray the house with flaming kerosene. Then turn down Rachel's sheet. Fluff the pillow against the wall and set out a nice book for her to read. Is everything understood? Can you manage without a disaster requiring the attention of the doctor and the fire brigade? What book would you like, Rachel dear?"

"I want a Cornish pasty with lots of spicy hot tomato sauce on it."

Rose rushed from the room but midway collided with a man-mountain. If you're seven and three-quarters and in full flight every man is a mountain.

"Oh, Daddy, Daddy," Rose shrieked, and grabbed his nearest leg. If he hadn't taken hold of the door frame she'd have pulled him down.

He'd been coming through from the front of the house, descending from room to room, each room built by himself a step lower on the hillside. The Alps they called it when they were going up to the front. The Dungeons they called it when they were going down to the back.

My goodness, but he had a strange look about him.

"Frank," snapped Auntie Lizzie, "you're late!"

"Dad," cried Rennie.

"Dad," cried Rachel. "Why were you down the mine?"

The cowardly terrier slunk under the kitchen table and from all viewpoints passed from sight.

Dad was flushed as if he'd been running, an activity most infrequent. He was short of breath, yet each word came as distinctly as a word ever could.

"Godfathers, Lizzie, what have you been doing with the gun?"

Auntie Lizzie started wagging a finger at him. "Where have you been while your daughter was in need? Fights going on all over town; Crawfords and Herberts and Hobsons. Those children at your feet bringing home news of it. Childish nonsense about a school bell. Your precious friend Hooke. Half the boys in town running wild. Your daughter an innocent victim in the middle of it."

"I see nothing I could've done."

"Your daughter chased through town by hooligans. And you say there's nothing you could've done. Who did your work? By whose intervention was it done? God forbid, but by that helpless drunk, Ole Roll. And where were you while that tragic man was protecting your child? Down that wretched mine entertaining yourself. Or up to some other mischief? Canvassing votes? That lost cause. I hope not. Your responsibility was here."

"For the life of me, Lizzie, what's that supposed to mean?"

"Exactly what I'm saying."

"You've lost your sense of proportion. I hear nothing that explains the gun, one end of which you barely know from the other. And for forty years you've seen all these people beating each other up, grown-ups and children alike. If you're talking about fights at school and school-boys and school bells and family feuds, nothing's new. It's older than you are."

Oh dear, thought Rachel. Is this because of me?

"You're most outrageously late, Frank. Someone had to look for her. Someone had to go. Halfway back to town across the paddocks while Rennie and Rose were left to fend for themselves. Not knowing what I'd find out there and still not knowing. The mess she's in."

"I see her."

"One wouldn't think so! And you ask why I went out with a gun!"

"I don't know what concerns me more. My daughter, or the gun. Would you know a bullet from a bean? I hope you're not about to tell me someone's shot."

"Of course no one's shot!"

"Lizzie... Oh, Lizzie dear, don't let's worry the

children. When did we differ over any matter of importance? It's all right, kids. It really is. Everyone's upset. It'll pass."

Auntie Lizzie drew a deep breath and Dad said, "Rachel. Does Eddie fit into this business in town?"

She felt the colour leave her cheeks.

She didn't know where to look.

"He was in the fight, I suppose."

"But not involved in this chasing business?"

"They were little kids. Little kids. Nine or ten."

"He didn't chase them off? Didn't protect you?"

It was awful. It was awful. She could hardly get her breath.

"He wasn't there. He wouldn't have known."

"You mean he'd gone by then?"

"I suppose so."

Auntie Lizzie said, "She could've been kidnapped. She could've been halfway to Arabia. You were needed and you weren't here. I was frightened and you weren't here."

"I'm sorry. It's not the way I would've had it. There was trouble at the mine."

"There's always trouble at the mine."

"Yes."

"Now take a good look at your daughter."

Dad said, "I *do* see her, Lizzie."

"No more lessons with the Misses Herbert. Tonight's the last. No more worries like this. You'll have to teach her yourself."

"I couldn't teach her the tin whistle."

"Irresponsible and insensitive women sending a child into the night without escort. Did you have to run half-way to Kingdom Come in the cold and the dark when you were thirteen? Never once. When school was over you walked with the rest of us into the next room. But does your child have the same security? I have been made aware that she does not. And where do we find her? Half past six at night and far from home. This child you love so dearly on Sundays when she brings you credit."

Dad detached Rose from his right leg and Rennie from his left arm. The flush had gone from him. So had his breathlessness. He had become pale. "Lizzie, I'm beginning to know I've had a hard day."

"A *hard* day, digging some fool of a hole? What of your daughter's predicament?"

"I have yet to hear of the predicament."

"If you'd take the trouble to look for yourself!"

"I have been doing so, Lizzie, constantly, but I know my daughter and I see nothing that a day won't heal."

"You see no such thing."

"She's not weeping. She's not performing. She's not throwing herself into my arms."

"I was weeping before," Rachel said, in a kind of mumble.

"I'm sure you were. At your age, I would've been too. Is there anything you should tell me?"

What do you say? What do you do? She shook her head.

"Shall I repeat the question?"

She was at the very edge of letting go, of telling him about Eddie Crawford, of telling all those terrible things that would've pinned his ears to the sides of his head.

And she almost said, "I've lost my school satchel too. And when they find it you'll never believe."

And she almost went on, "I nearly got killed."

And she almost added, "It was an adventure like you never had, I bet you. I was very brave."

Instead, aloud, mumbled lamely, "I called and you didn't come."

And as an afterthought she very nearly said, "When the crippled boy hollered, you went through fire. When I hollered, you didn't hear."

He was giving her a puzzled look that disconcerted her more and more. "You know I couldn't come. The mine's our living. It's not a fool hole in the ground. I was too far away to hear. Ole Roll, you say. Ole Roll did what for you?"

"The boys. The young kids in the high street. They chased me and Ole Roll was going home the wrong way. He shooed the boys off. He went for them with his cane. He took care of me. He said it was too late for me to be out. He said I was to tell you. He said he might tell you himself."

"I hear you. I hear you. . . You said he was going the wrong way?"

"I told him he ought to go the other way. I told him it was going to be cold. I think he borrowed a horse to go home quicker."

"What makes you think that?"

"I heard him pass."

"A pity you didn't hail him. If he'd taken care of you once, he might have taken care of you again."

It was on the tip of her tongue and almost out — "That's what I said to Eddie!" But she stopped it! By an instant! By a missed heartbeat! Oh, to be sharp was so hard when you were so tired and were only guessing at what he knew.

Breathlessly, she said, "He was too far away. He wouldn't have heard. He was singing."

"This, I take it," said Dad, "would have been some time ago? An hour ago?"

"It couldn't have been an hour ago," Rachel said miserably, knowing, just knowing, that keeping Eddie out of trouble might be more than she'd be able to do.

"It was an hour ago," Dad said, and seemed to run out of words. Seemed not to know which way to go. He looked to Auntie Lizzie and shook his head, and went on shaking his head, then said, "Lizzie, I know you've cooked a lovely dinner. You've filled the house with the smells of it. We're all in need of it. I think I'm dying for it. What about you, Rachel?"

She raised her head and he was smiling back at her. Perhaps wanly. Oh my goodness, what did he know?

"Yes, Dad," she said. "Dinner."

"Fine," he said. "A mature decision. But let's have a clean-up first. And let's see the table set fit for the king. Please, Lizzie, make the effort. With the gun, if you don't mind, removed to the front room and the key turned."

As for Rachel, he was keeping it, she knew. Keeping it on ice, as it were. Keeping what?

She was so tired. So tired.

CHAPTER TWELVE

Dad's Sunday-best Suit

The dinner table was set fit for the king. Well, fit for these his humble subjects, on the opposite side of the world from the royal palace, this 14 July, Friday, Election Eve.

A starched linen cloth concealing all but the legs of the scrubbed pine table and a sideways glimpse of the cautiously projecting nose of the cowardly terrier, whose unaccustomed presence in the house appeared to have been forgotten.

Upon the cloth, two tall glasses of rich new milk, one for Rennie and the other for Rose, fresh from the cow but two hours. Not for Rachel though. Most definitely never. Most categorically no.

"Milk," said Rachel at an early age, the statement being reported by her father's younger sister, "is for making cheese."

Hence, a jug of new rainwater, fresh from Heaven but two days.

Condiments and sauces in variety also upon the table; plum sauce, tomato sauce, pepper sauce, Worcestershire sauce, even English mustard, wet-mixed, very yellow, very hot, not so deadly as to discourage Rachel's daring, but deadly enough in moments of forgetfulness to knock her witless and speechless.

If you fancy adult pleasures, you pay the adult price.

Flowers also upon the dinner table; sprays of wild heath from the hillside across the creek and, beside Dad's place, one General Jack French rose out of season; a bud, a teardrop, a ruby. In view of recent events, which left Auntie Lizzie strongly perturbed, she almost didn't put it there.

Another fruit plate, for the first had vanished in the darkness outside, Tomorrow, perhaps, they'd find it a few steps off the path, or under the dairy where snakes had been known to hide in summer. The tiger snakes. The snakes which were rumoured, when angry, to rear upon their tails in open country and pursue children faster than a child could run. Snakes as tall as a man, on their tails, in pursuit. Awful.

A gleaming white tureen. Lovely, lovely pea soup. Waiting. Steaming. As thick as rapture.

Mmmmmmmm.

Rachel, though scratched and scraped and sore, came out clean and faintly shining, as instructed by Dad some minutes before, his bellow coming from his bedroom in the Alps.

"I'll have all three of you, smart, clean, and shining. Dressed in your best. Do you hear? No argument."

To which Auntie Lizzie protested, "Do I have nothing to do with my time but sponge and wash and scrub and starch and iron?"

To which Dad replied, "With crisp white pinafores to catch the spills and crumbs."

To which Auntie Lizzie protested, "I'm not dressing up three children to sit at a workaday table. Do you see me with a dozen hands?"

To which Dad replied, "I see them with hands of their own. The master hath spoken."

Out of which Rennie and Rose emerged nervously in the dresses reserved for church and Rachel in her best nightie, and Auntie Lizzie, with one hand to her brow and the other to the small of her aching back, issued the command, "Napkins round your necks and towels across your laps and if one stain gets through, woe to you."

Dad came down in his Sunday-best suit.

Auntie Lizzie's face lengthened.

"Glory be," she said. "Haven't we suffered enough?"

Oh *dear*, thought Rachel.

He's got his suit on.

I don't think I can stand it on top of everything.

What's he got his suit on for when it's only Friday?

Dad stood at the head of the table, resplendent, in a modest, inexpensive, mail-order way, Rachel stepping in apprehensively on his right side, Rennie and Rose just as apprehensively on his left, and Auntie Lizzie, after a hard day, beginning to look more and more despondent at the opposite end, the foot, the position described by herself as the doormat.

"This," Dad said, in reply to Auntie Lizzie, "is your brother dressed to kill."

"I'd noticed," she said.

"Who are you going to kill, Dad?" Rose asked. "The boys who chased Rachel up the street? If you kill them too hard you'll get blood on your suit."

Dad turned sternly to Rose and pressed a finger to his lips. Then he turned to Rachel with a frown. "What's the nightdress for, young lady?"

"To go to bed in, Dad."

"It was my instruction," said Auntie Lizzie, "to an exhausted child, before you entered the house."

"Oh," said Dad, and bowed his head.

All heads bowed, as was the custom. All eyes closed.

Well, Rachel's eyes closed, and she never peeped, not tonight or any other night, for peeping was sinning and God would mark an entry against her in the big black book. But she thought Rennie might have peeped from time to time to check up on the others in a strictly practical way. But Rose was so beautiful she could do anything. Peep to her heart's content. God wouldn't mind. Rose could ask leading questions. Dad wouldn't mind, only say, "Isn't she a duck!" Rose could be the tiniest bit cheeky when Dad came down in his Sunday-best suit. And in return receive a very stern look that actually said, "You're a delight. You're gorgeous. My darling child, what would I do without you?" And everyone was in agreement.

"Heavenly Father," Dad said for the 4792nd time in Rachel's presence, "we thank Thee for all Thy mercies; help us to eat and drink to Thy glory; to enjoy the sleep of the just; to rise gladly to the morrow; to work always with a will. Amen."

Whereupon he took his seat and all thankfully followed, even Auntie Lizzie, who at once served the lovely, lovely pea soup in the silence of hope, dropping into each bowl a measure of diced bread which bobbed perkily on top. With a little imagination you could hear the bread crackle, for Auntie Lizzie had fried it quickly, crisp and golden, in the very best beef dripping.

Ooh aah, thought Rachel, inhaling deeply. And what wonderful medicine it was. A good sniff was second-best only to a good swallow.

But oh agony, thought Rachel, he's just got to get on with spooning it up. Please, God, I'm sure you know him even better than we do. You know he can't be trusted when he puts that suit on. It does awful things to him. Why would he put it on tonight? Isn't Sunday teatime enough for us kids without getting it on Fridays as well? Specially a Friday like today. Do we really need sermons from Dad? You must know he's never given a good one yet. His Christmas Day message for 1904. Did you ever hear anything like it? I'll bet you put a black mark in his book. If you didn't, I did.

Dad, meanwhile, was saying, "My mother had the first tent with a proper glass window on the Ballarat goldfields. I know that's not news to you, but I'm reminding you. That was my father. That was distinction. That was flair. That brought people around to stare and to ask the question 'Are we here only to strip the land bare or adorn it?' Because of him we live as we do."

Dad spoke much slower than Rachel did her thinking.

It'd kill you stone dead, she thought. He's horrible. He knows I'm hungry enough to eat the leg off the table. He doesn't care. He's worse than the preacher. The

preacher's supposed to preach. Dad's supposed to be a
mining engineer. Why tonight? It's not fair.

"My father used to say," said Dad, "that discipline in
the home is the privilege and the obligation of the man.
The children are not to be consulted; they are to be told.
The man gives commands, not reasons. Reasons are for
the child to find in his own good time. Man, he used to
say, when it is time to eat, is not an animal at the pig
trough."

I think I am though, Rachel thought, especially tonight, after getting the life scared out of me, after saving Eddie Crawford from that hole, after running like a
racehorse for farther than the Melbourne Cup. After getting worn down to my bootlaces. I think my good time for
reasons is a long way off.

Dad said, "In my father's opinion — and that opinion
came direct from all the generations that preceded him —
the child who broke the rules of the table broke the law.
The law of the house. The law of the family. Just as the
thief breaks the law of property. And the murderer breaks
the law of life's sanctity. And headstrong boys and girls
often break the laws of waiting until life is ready to give up
its mysteries in proper time. Offenders against all laws, my
father used to say, must expect and accept punishment
in just measure, or civilisation becomes a nothing, a mere
veneer that peels off. But he was a good man. He was a
fair man. He was kind."

Oh dear, Rachel groaned inside. What's he doing to
me? What's he saying? I think he's ahead of me or something. I don't know whether he's getting at me or not.
Why can't he let me eat my dinner?

"We're but a little lower than the angels, our father
told us. A great responsibility. We were never to succumb
to the common urge. Never to be less than what we ought
to be. And told our half-brothers and sisters the same,
I'm sure, in later years, after our mother died and we
went away to Mrs Fairchild's school in Happy Valley."

It's shaping up to be a history lesson, Rachel groaned inside. I just know. It'll last for hours. The soup'll go cold. Everything'll spoil. He should've been a teacher, then he could've worn his suit every day and not got so excited about putting it on.

"Even if we live in a hut on the fringe of the wilderness, our father used to say, we uphold the dignity of the table. God intended us to eat with refinement and appreciation, to approach with poise each meal prepared for us by loving hands, not to come to the table like barbarians about to tear everything to ribbons with our teeth."

I don't know what he's up to, Rachel groaned inside. Is he telling me something I've got to know? All that talk about getting on with our dinner. About dying for it. Dying for it is right.

"In Guernsey, years and years ago, my father's family was much respected. And for all I know, still is. They built ships. They sailed their own ships. All my father did was dig holes. Was pursue the El Dorado. But he was respected here because he went on meeting the just expectations of his fellow men. Even at the Stockade at Eureka in 1854. But no hero's grave for him when his time came. Or a gold-plated one. Up the road he lies in my nightshirt."

That's fairly widely known, Rachel thought, round here, and he got to sixty-two, didn't he? A reasonable share. I'll be lucky to get to fourteen if I don't eat my dinner. And this fellow who's trying to give the impression he knows everything is taking a very serious risk with his own dinner. Any moment there could be a knocking at the door, Eddie's father with a handful of Eddie's hair, Eddie getting dragged behind. If Mr Hothead Crawford turns up here that'll be the stone end.

"That second family of my father's," Dad said, "was a large one. Never a serious numerical challenge to the Hobsons, the Herberts and the Crawfords, but a challenge at home just the same, the feeding of them, the clothing of them, the housing of them. Not much left for himself. But they couldn't bury him in his old grey underwear. That wouldn't have done. So they came to this door asking if I had a nice white nightshirt to dress him for his journey. Never found his El Dorado. Never built his stately home. Never came into his family inheritance. Just choked his life out in the dust of other men's mines."

Perhaps it was because Dad was going into politics. Perhaps it was the election. Life might be like this from now on. Councillor Frank Lefevre Junior wearing his Sunday-best suit for dinner every night, even though his own father didn't possess one. Practising his speeches on his sister and kids. Dinner going cold. Everyone fainting from hunger.

Rachel sneaked a glance at Auntie Lizzie. You'd have thought she'd been hit on the head and was still recovering. Then Rachel sneaked a glance across to Rennie who made as if to show the whites of her eyes, but thought the better of it. And beside Rennie, Rose solemnly bit on her lower lip, as if to say, "I'm sorry about this. I'm real embarrassed my dad's going on like this."

"But my father," Dad said, "insisted upon a properly set table, as you see here. Thank you for the rose, Lizzie dear. And none of us ate before he ate. And none of us spoke without his permission. And all of us at the table behaved — visibly and invisibly — as if the Queen had come. All the way to Melbourne and beyond households of Lefevres are trying in every way to do things right because of him. So who's to say his life of failure was not a triumph?"

Rose dropped her eyes to her lap and Rennie looked straight ahead as if someone had just run a point into her back and Rachel thought, "Something's coming, I'm sure, I'm sure. I can feel it in my bones."

"Tall oaks from little acorns grow," Dad said, looking a most serious Auntie Lizzie directly in the eye, and shaking his head. He turned to Rachel then and said, "As you, my daughter, also are about to know, for an elderly person of recent acquaintance has need of my nightshirt." Whereupon Dad took a sip of soup.

Rachel heard the words several times, put them together several times, then knew what Dad had said.

Ole Roll's dead.

Dad hadn't used the words, and hadn't explained, but that's what he had said as he had raised his spoon and passed it across the surface of his bowl, then in silence conveyed a modest tasting to his mouth.

Ole Roll's dead.

Isn't that sad? So suddenly. So soon. Isn't it strange? You make a sort of friend where you wouldn't have looked for one. Just as suddenly everything's gone.

Because Eddie busted Willie's nose? Perhaps. Because she'd warned him he was going the wrong way? Perhaps. Because he stole a horse to get home before the cold? Perhaps. But how did Dad know? Had Ole Roll gone to him and told? He'd said it! He'd said that he would!

"How?" she cried across the table.

In silence, at this time, Dad swallowed his modest tasting of Auntie Lizzie's soup. An accomplishment not lost upon Rachel, even then, for every time she tried to swallow in silence like a lady (or a gentleman) it went down the wrong way and provoked a nasty situation.

"Most excellent soup, Lizzie dear," Dad said, "and not in the least cold."

"I'm pleased to hear it. You mean these bewildered children may begin?"

"Well yes. Why not?" Dad smiled across at Rachel and said, "In the dam. At the mine. From the horse. Thrown. On the way to speak to me, I suppose, for which you must never feel the blame. Pea soup on a cold night. One of the nice things about coming home."

Inside, Rachel said, "Poor Ole Roll. I'm sure his life wasn't a triumph even though it was a failure... I don't know. I'm sad. I'm sorry. But that pea soup does look good. Looks so good. Ten thousand times thank you for pea soup that tastes so good..."

"Real, real good," Rennie said.

Pea soup fit for kings and angels and for fugitives from Eddie Crawford and his hoodlums. New life. New hope. A new view of the world. And there needed to be, because trying to make sense of that old world out there...

"Oh, my," Rose said to her empty bowl.

For everyone, even Dad, there was a generous second measure. "Lizzie," he said. "It is. Most excellent. I wonder whether you've surpassed yourself."

"I doubt it. I'd be surprised if it's more than ordinary. Everyone's waited so long they wouldn't know fish from fowl."

Rachel smiled. A wanness, a weariness, a warmth, and went on smiling, barely knowing.

How I love my Auntie Lizzie. I know it's a very thin joke, like most of my jokes, but it's true: the only thing better than a bowl of her pea soup is two bowls. Though it's also true I do wish she wouldn't leave mutton strips warmed over in the oven for breakfast. Perhaps tomorrow, with the election and all, being Saturday and all, and everyone having had such a terrible time tonight, we might get fried potatoes.

At which point Auntie Lizzie presented the Cornish pasties with a kind of self-effacing shyness. Yet with an underlying confidence, a conviction, a pride, for she knew that good food healed.

Healing it might have been, but torture, too, for the family, as she carefully conveyed them from the oven, five superlative pasties by some miracle still perfect beyond description, though held over for three-quarters of an hour.

Poor Ole Roll. Did he ever, ever, come home to Cornish pasties?

If he'd lived a bit longer, perhaps he could've come, some Friday, for tea.

Rachel's sad eyes met her dad's.

Oh, those Cornish pasties, each, with the exception of
the largest, a little smaller than the others, the difference
between them never disheartening even the youngest, all
steaming with the fragrance of hillside gardens and spices
from the Orient and delights almost beyond the reach of
the imagination. And large. Elegantly large. Not in any
way gross. Each, for its intended, a feast.

Auntie Lizzie, thought Rachel, no one in the world is
more beautiful than you. You can growl at me any time
you like because I know you love me all the time. I just
know, just for tonight, the second biggest will be mine.
(Please, God, in case Auntie Lizzie has anything else in
mind, can it be arranged?) Oh, Auntie Lizzie, I wish I
were an artist so I could paint you. I'd paint you like a
saint with a halo round your head, and an inscription at
the bottom, *St Elizabeth, Rachel's Auntie, Champion
Cook of the World*. And they'd hang it in the gallery
at Ballarat and come from all around to say, "She cooks
pasties. You've never seen pasties like them unless you live
in her house. They're better than Heinze's pork sausages,
which are only sausages after all, and made for profit, not
for love."

Oh, Auntie Lizzie, is that gorgeous pasty, beyond all
description, really for me? Thank you, God, thank you,
thank you, for arranging it. I'll be so good after this for
such a long time.

Oh, Auntie Lizzie, I know it was yours, I know you've
given it to me. Thank you. Thank you. And with your
extra special tomato sauce with red pepper, and black
pepper, and cloves. Then with nice hot cups of tea to
wash it down.

Dad said, "Before we begin..."

Rachel heard, but didn't want to believe.

Rachel stared, that her lovely father could be so cruel.

Rachel's breath caught, to choke off the words.

Dad said, "Tonight's been uncommonly rough for
some of us. And uncommonly rough for others we know.

Not only large streams from little fountains flow, and tall oaks from little acorns grow, but big troubles from small causes can send us off in directions we'd never intended to go. So... So, friends, Romans and countrymen, you'll observe I'm dressed for leaving the house. Not for a moment have I considered that at this late stage, at this last ditch, from the edge of this brink of predictable defeat, that a public appearance this evening with my handsome family might possibly bring me a few welcome votes. Might possibly turn the tide against that dreadful fellow, that liar, that scoundrel, that bully, in whose presence I fear I may spit... Nevertheless... Nevertheless... After you finish your dinner, Rachel Elizabeth, I'd like to see that nightdress put aside and your Sunday-best put on. And Rennie and Rose, you two boys will clear the table and stack the dishes ready for washing in the morning."

"Never," cried Auntie Lizzie. "Dirty dishes left lying will bring the filthy mice."

"God's creatures all," said Dad.

"We've got all night to wash the dishes," cried Auntie Lizzie. "The church social is next week!"

Dad said, "Nice warm head scarves on the lot of you. Your pale-green velvet gown, Lizzie, is the most becoming. And a blanket for everyone's lap. Tonight at eight-thirty in the public hall I'm proposing we shall witness Mrs Ernest Headstone of Sacramento, USA... I ask you, imagine living in a town with a name like that... To here she has come. To this place. To this dump. I cannot bring myself to utter its name in company so illustrious. Tonight, in this place, we shall be present to hear Mrs Ernest Headstone deliver her world-famous lecture, with magic lantern slides and practical demonstration, 'Your Future in Your Bumps', even if that ape Hobson is in charge of proceedings. That's what I say. What say you?"

In awe, Rose cried, "I've never, never, never gone out at night before, except to something at the church."

And Rennie, forgetting she would be eleven before long, said, "Oh, Daddy."

And Auntie Lizzie said, "Headstrong. Mrs Ernest Headstrong."

And Rachel said, "All this and pasties too." But to herself, so no one could hear, she added, "If Mr Hothead comes knocking at this door before we get away, I'll die."

CHAPTER THIRTEEN

Full Circle

Was it a magic time that tucked itself away in between, a bit of enchantment that Rachel knew was there, but wasn't able to grasp. It was as if she was almost in it, but not quite. She was far too weary from aches and pains and recent efforts of will and nerve.

She didn't even envy Rennie and Rose the clear, bright, excited place where they bubbled like soda water. Bubbled round about each other and bubbled over.

Bed would have been so good. But there in a moment she'd have gone to no one knew where; nothing to be found but an exhausted young body from which the spirit had flown; gone until tomorrow; no lady to read bumps; no lantern magic; no supper afterwards in the hall.

An enchanted time. All the family glowing with good-will. Everyone feeling rotund, full of lovely pea soup and superlative pasties washed down by nice hot cups of tea. Rachel wandering through the house as if alone, with an eye on the hands of the hurrying clock and an ear to the door. Every moment anxious, so wearing, so wearying, but warm.

No knocking at that door. No raised voice out there. No angry man with a handful of Eddie's hair.

The relief of that. The unwinding.

Oh, it would have been lovely in bed, to drift away, but how lovely it would be to drive to town in the buggy and pair under the stars.

Rachel fighting against herself, smiling, striving to remain awake, stumbling over steps and colliding with the sides of doors, and, for a moment out of sight of the others, slapping herself in the face.

"What was that? What was that?" Auntie Lizzie calling sharply.

"Just me, Auntie Lizzie. Nothing at all."

The night outside wasn't an enemy any more. The cold wasn't cruel. The damp and brooding dark that began in the bushlands and reached out into all the world had been overcome by the clean black night from the stars.

Everyone rugged up from the tips of the toes to the bridge of the nose and the sharp cold striking at your eyebrows was like an alarm clock.

Time to wake up, Rachel!

Everyone sitting up in the buggy, front seat and back, almost as if the "Wedding March" were about to play, for there wasn't a smarter vehicle this side of town, nor a more handsome pair of ponies.

Elegance was a state of mind, as Dad might say, like being rich or being poor. Once you wore the mark you took it with you everywhere, head held high, a sparkle in your eye, and your two big toes beating time.

When Dad first drove that elegant buggy in through the gate, Billy and Larry looking so splendid, Auntie Lizzie came out of the house uncharacteristically with a voice they heard next door at the Hobsons', whose block was far enough away on a misty day to be out of sight. "You've borrowed it, I hope!"

"No."

"Borrowed the ponies then, at least."

"No."

"On appraisal, I trust, buggy and ponies, to be returned to Ballarat expressing your extreme dissatisfaction first thing Monday morning."

"No."

"You're out of your mind."

"Yes."

"It's beyond our means. What's your job but managing a tin-pot hole in the ground? What do you own of it but eighty shares? A buggy as long as a landau. Fifty pounds, if it cost a penny."

"As usual, Lizzie, on every count you're so right."

"You'll attract the thieves. They'll think we're a honey-pot. They'll waylay us on the road. They'll think the Celebration's struck it rich. The company, Heaven forbid, may think you're fiddling the books."

"It's a spiritual experience, Lizzie dear. Above money or price. Every time we take it out you'll agree. You'll see."

Within the week she ungrudgingly conceded the point. "It's spiritual," she said.

Rachel agreed from the start, though in the dark, as now, little of the splendour showed, except the glow of lamp glasses and the gleam of brass, and sparks like stars struck by hooves on the white quartz road, stars above and stars below, as if you drove through the heavens themselves along the Milky Way.

Oh, the jangling and the jingling and the clip-clopping and the crunching of the gravel and the excitement tingling deep down. Spasms of wakefulness in Rachel now as well as spasms of fatigue.

Your Future in Your Bumps.

How wonderful was the world.

"She reads your head," Rennie said, "like it's got words printed on it."

"Where'd you hear that?" scoffed Rose. "You've got words on *your* head, I think. *Rennie is a donkey.*"

"We've all got words on our heads but you've got to know where to look. The lady knows. I'm not allowed to tell how I know, because it's secret."

"If it's secret no one would've told you."

"They told me because I'm trustworthy," Rennie said. "Not like you, Rose Lefevre, chattering all over the place like a chickowee. Looks at your head, she does, ever so close. I hope you washed your hair, Rose. I hope you don't disgrace us with tangles and knots and things."

Jangling on towards town, gravel crunching, lovely rhythm of the ponies, heard and just seen, and in Rachel a new and strong spasm of nervousness, for back from the road there they were, the lights of the Crawford house.

That terrible Eddie Crawford. The trouble he's caused. The trouble still to come. May his sums go wrong. May he forget how to spell. May his bagpipes explode. May all the people leap to their feet and boo. Though it's true, of course, I *am* going to town to hear the lovely lady and if Eddie hadn't chased me, who knows?

"Activity in the Crawford house," Dad said. "What's going on there?"

And that's the trouble, Rachel thought, markedly retreating, neck shortening, legs shortening, arms shortening, eyes shutting tight. No one knows what anyone knows, only knows their own little bit.

"Perhaps," said Auntie Lizzie, "the Crawfords have changed their minds like us about staying home. Perhaps they're coming in to get their heads read, too."

"I'd hope so," Dad said. "How many Crawfords are there round here? Like the stars without number. Every one of them needing his or her head read as a kind of public duty."

Auntie Lizzie raised her voice. "No child heard that vulgarity. And no child will repeat it. Or we'll lose the few friends we have."

Rachel shrinking yet farther into her seat fearing that Mr Hothead was about to come rushing out of his house waving a couple of bricks.

Everyone knew he was a terribly bad-tempered fellow. Chrissie said the only safe place to be when he got up steam was a long way off. Not that she'd ever seen him in the act of chewing anyone up. Her big brothers told her, particularly Gregor, the axeman, who told her about most things, Gregor being the sort of fellow who enjoyed spinning a yarn. Not that Gregor had seen his father performing at his wildest either, Gregor being too good-natured to provoke anyone to anger. Gregor got it from his grandfather, the one known as the Crawford on the Hill, who watched over the district like an old owl sitting up a gum tree. Very like Gregor; loved spinning a yarn. Knew everything about everybody and bore the wounds to prove it. Like the paralysed right hand got forty years ago from trying to bash the temper out of Chrissie's dad.

The Crawford house was gone.

Rachel opened her eyes and no lights were to be seen. Lovely, lovely. And no wild man was rushing along behind throwing bricks.

"Reading the bumps on the heads of people," Dad said from up front, "is a serious scientific study of the cranium built upon the accumulated wisdom and observations of the ages, going back to the dawn of time. One of Adam's first jobs was reading Eve's bumps."

"That's more than enough of that," said Auntie Lizzie. "Remember who you are and where you are and what you hope to be tomorrow!"

"The cranium," said Dad, "for the benefit of you boys in the back seat, varies from race to race, from flat to high and broad to narrow and smooth to rough and back to front, the latter classification referring largely to the Hobson family as manifested in these parts."

"You will ignore your father," said Auntie Lizzie. "He's very wicked and he knows it."

My father, thought Rachel, wouldn't know how to be wicked. He's beautiful.

"In the case of each race," said Dad, "the cranium varies from person to person in the way that noses do. What's the nose, anyway, but a bump with a couple of holes in it stuck on the forward-facing surface instead of the upward-facing surface? All other bumps, such as those got from falling on your head off rooftops, have no permanent bearing upon the ones that really count, that determine your future and reveal it to the sensitive hands of an informed person like Mrs Headstone."

"Headstrong," said Auntie Lizzie.

"Whatever you say," said Dad. "The bumps that really count being those that you're born with, or the ones you acquire along the way from using your brain to excess or not using it at all. The next exception being complicated forms of concussion, the size of hen eggs, from which you wake up in the next world, such as being hit on the bean with a hard-driven cricket ball or some ruffian's shillelagh; people that read bumps not commonly being asked to deal with bumps of this kind, they being more usually the province of sawbones who pronounce their judgements in terms less interested in events of a future kind. The science of reading bumps is called phrenology. Isn't that so, Lizzie?"

"For Heaven's sake, why ask me? I know nothing of these matters. I can't even say the word. What time at nights do I have to read books like other people I know? I spend my nights washing dishes and darning socks with big toe holes in them and patching and stitching and putting the chief offenders to bed."

"We put ourselves to bed," Rose cried. "We wash the dishes, too."

"You might do the washing," Auntie Lizzie said, "and sometimes a smudge of the drying, but I do the worrying and that's the hard part. What you're going to break next and how we're going to pay for it. Your father never with a penny to bless himself. Always putting it in some fool goldmine. If it's a hole in the ground he throws his money down it. Everyone between here and Ballarat knows he's a soft touch. If they've got a hole to dig whose door do they run to knock on? Always losing his shirt or giving it away."

"He's got two shirts, Auntie Lizzie," Rose said. "One on and a spare in the wardrobe."

"He's got three," Rennie said, "if you count the one he puts on the scarecrow."

Or four, thought Rachel, until tomorrow, if you include his nightshirt.

Poor Ole Roll. He never had anything like this, did he? Living on his own. He never drove into town under the stars. He never had fun. He never had games.

"When we speak of shirts," Dad explained, "we speak metaphorically. Don't we, Lizzie? Shirts not meaning shirts in a practical sense. Only in a metaphorical sense."

"I wouldn't know the meaning of the word. You're addressing a woman stupefied by hard work. Poor old brain worn down like an old boot. Phrenology and metaphorically. Can't even pronounce them."

"You just pronounced them," Rose shrieked.

"No, I didn't. Your ears are playing tricks. It's known as sleight of hearing."

"It's Rennie who's got slight of hearing," cried Rose. "I *heard*. Didn't you hear her, Dad?"

"Quiet, you people in the back," said Dad. "You'll frighten the horses."

I didn't think I was making a noise, Rachel thought. I thought I was just thinking.

Rose was shrieking, "I won't frighten the horses. If I jumped up and down and screamed at them they'd only laugh. Heehaw. Heehaw. Same as Rennie does. Same as Rachel does. Same as you do. Everybody laughs at me."

I'm not laughing, Rachel thought. I don't hear myself laughing. Do you? I'm just sitting here minding my own business, trying to stay awake. It's like being in a boat. Like being down at Geelong again on our holiday. Like rocking on the waves. It would've been nice to have stayed home in bed. I'd have dreamt of sails and sunsets and nice boys with golden hair paddling canoes. Wouldn't have been worrying about that horrible Eddie Crawford.

Rennie said, "I'd like to hear the lady say I'm not going to be deaf all my life. If you get the scarlet fever everyone brings you grapes. If you get the slight of hearing they yell at you and call you a dunce. It's not funny having slight of hearing."

"You manage very well," Dad said, "and I'm proud of you."

"We've got someone following," Rose cried. "I can see his lights. Lots of lights."

Rachel's heart started jumping so hard she felt it against her ribs. The Crawfords. The Crawfords.

"It's a public road," Dad said. "He's allowed to follow if he wants to. And behind him there might be another following on, too. It's called traffic, Rose Lefevre, namely, and in general, the progression without prior consultation of assorted human agencies on wheels or hooves moving in file in one direction or another."

Rose sniffed. "He's always saying things I don't understand. He does it on purpose. I hope the traffic's a bushranger with a big gun to give him a good scare."

"If it is," Dad said, "we'll fix him. He can have you. In no time at all he won't know what day it is and he'll shoot himself by mistake."

"I have such a rude father," Rose said. "The things he says to me he'd never say to anyone bigger because they'd hit him on the head and then the lady wouldn't know what bumps to read."

Rachel was sighing and coming up again for air. All was well. It really was. There wasn't any talk of Crawfords. It was good being there. Having Rose around was like living with good news.

Then Rennie said, "I'd like to hear the lady say I'm going to have twelve children when I grow up, one for every month of the year, so we can have lots of birthday parties."

"Heaven help us," said Auntie Lizzie.

Rose shrilled, "Well, I hope she says I'm not going to have twelve children. I wouldn't know where to put them."

"Send them off to school all day," said Rennie, "and let Mr Hooke worry about that, then put them to work round the house at night."

"The way you get put to work, I suppose," Auntie Lizzie said.

Rennie gave but brief thought to that, then said, "On

Saturdays they can chop wood to sell to all the people and on Sundays and holidays they can come to visit you so you can hear their multiplication tables."

"Thank you for the kindness," said Auntie Lizzie. "It's a comfort I'll be looking forward to in my old age."

I don't know, Rachel thought, drifting somewhere nearby, after everything awful that's happened tonight, after a real dark page, you turn it over and stars come bursting out from everywhere, like the bonfire in Herberts' paddock on Empire night when the dry sticks catch and up it goes.

A real genuine night out in town. Perhaps with people you hardly ever saw. New people to see. New people to meet. Different from the ones in church every week. Different from the ones at school. Getting driven there in style, and a lady from Sacrasomewhere waiting to tell you about your very own personal bumps, about your very own future, as if you were really going to have one after all.

Not so long ago it looked like your future was about to fall in a heap. But it hadn't. It didn't turn bad and it didn't drop dead. It turned good instead.

Some futures ended. Others had new beginnings.

There's magic in it. There really is, real magic, this guessing at what's lying out there in wait, as if it's a road that's still to come into view.

Rachel thinking of that road, and smiling. Thinking of it and going far, far away.

There she'd be, ten years on, twenty years on — goodness, goodness, how could it be? — walking the length of that road, her very own life happening all around. Sunshine or rain? Sunshine, please.

Rachel, glamorous and grown-up in gorgeous clothes — twirling a parasol when no one else was looking. Not very likely though.

Rachel writing her own music? Getting it onto paper so she could keep it to play another day?

Rachel at the manual of an organ as big as a room? A pipe organ. Please. All the people leaping to their feet and clapping hands when they should've stood in an orderly fashion to sing a hymn.

Rachel in a bridal gown? Yes. Standing beside whom?

Not Eddie Crawford if she could help it. He'd ruined his chances. Along with all his cousins, Herberts, Crawfords, or Hobsons, who'd ruined their chances too, ages ago.

"I hope," Rachel said out loud, "that when she reads my head she's going to find lots of songs written there, written on the inside, too, all nice and clear, so I can see them, and play them again later when I want to. I get real cross having all these lovely tunes going round in my head. I get so cross when I can't remember the ones I played yesterday. There must be something wrong with my brain, I think."

"Get the lady to fix it," said Rose. "Perhaps she'll have a little hammer. Ask her to hit you with it."

"I'll ask her to hit you."

Well, thought Rachel, that was a smart enough response. Rose might be knee-high to a grasshopper but keeping up with her was a struggle.

"This evening," said Auntie Lizzie, "I'm expecting three impeccably behaved young Lefevres to remain silent and attentive while Mrs Headstrong addresses us, and particularly when the lights are turned low for the magic lantern. Then, if Mrs Headstrong chooses not to read their bumps, but restricts her demonstrations to proper grown-up people, no protest will be voiced by these young Lefevres until they're on the way home again and thoroughly out of earshot of anyone who could convey their dissatisfaction back again. Keeping your opinions of other people to yourselves — particularly if they're not flattering — is a practice I earnestly commend. As life progresses you'll discover how wise your old aunt is. Furthermore, said aunt expects these young Lefevres to eat a fair share of supper only, accepting tea if it's offered, but declining coffee courteously. Coffee, like sitting up late, is for proper grown-up people. You hear me, Rose? Rose, particularly. Do you hear?"

"Yes, Auntie Lizzie."

"Rennie? Particularly Rennie also?"

"Yes, Auntie Lizzie."

"And you, Rachel Lefevre, against whom this admonition is most particularly addressed?"

"Auntie Lizzie, you know I'd never drink coffee against your wishes."

"Do I really know that? I hope so."

"This doesn't mean," Dad said, "that you're not allowed to laugh a little if it's funny or dab a tear from your eye if it's sad. Isn't that so, Lizzie?"

"Moderation in all things, brother dear. They'll need to ask our permission."

"Oh, absolutely. That's understood, I'm sure."

"By golly," cried Rennie, "we might as well have stayed home and done our homework."

"They're teasing," Rachel said, pleased that she was awake enough to pick the difference between fact and fancy.

"Teasing?" Auntie Lizzie's voice went up the scale. "Going out to have a good time is a very serious business. Isn't that so, Frank? For if one misbehaves troubles must follow. Beatings. Confinement to rooms without lunch or dinner. Extra dishes to wash. Extra logs to bring up from the woodheap."

"Absolutely," agreed Dad. "Troubles that bring pain to us all, but much more pain to you boys than to us."

"They're always teasing when they're in a good mood," Rachel said. "They shouldn't tease little girls. They forget little girls don't understand."

"I'm not a little girl," protested Rennie.

"Nor am I," shrilled Rose. "I'm big. I'm seven and three-quarters."

"There you are," said Dad. "They know what the situation really is. When you want the truth ask a child. As for Auntie Lizzie and me, we were almost known as the Terrible Twins, though for some reason we weren't."

"That's because you were known as the Terrible Fibbers," Rachel said, and began to wonder whether she was in a kind of continuing delirium, still in the bushlands, trapped in the hole, quartz rubble over her head.

The buggy turned the corner to join the straight stretch into town. Or appeared to. More spasms of wakefulness. More spasms of fatigue. The rhythm of the ponies and the crunching of the wheels.

Streetlamps glowing a long way apart; the yellow flicker of another vehicle a distinct distance ahead; half a dozen or more people nearby sharing a light, hastening on foot, someone calling as the buggy passed, "It's Rachel! Hullo." Rachel calling back, "Hullo," and wondering who it was. Sitting up to glance back. Thinking of Mary Riley. Hoping it was someone else. Then thinking, that's not fair. That's not nice. It's not Mary's fault.

"Busy tonight, by George," Dad said. "All these people. You know, I remember when 25,000 souls lived hereabouts."

"I see more people at church," Rose said. "I don't think you can count."

"He's teasing," Rennie said, as if to say, "I'm ten, and understand; you're seven, and don't."

"No one can tell properly when he's teasing," Rose said. "He can't tell himself."

To which Dad rejoined, "Out of the mouths of babes and sucklings."

"I'm not a suckling," Rose protested. "A suckling's a little pig."

"I see nothing to argue about," said Dad.

"He's at it again," Rose cried. "Why's he always making a fool of me?"

"Because you got born into the family," Auntie Lizzie said. "He wouldn't have bothered otherwise."

"I should've got born into some other family."

"You wouldn't have had Dad at all then," Rennie said, "or Auntie Lizzie. Or Auntie Susie. You mightn't even have known them."

"True," said Dad, "and you wouldn't have known Rennie or Rachel either."

Rose sniffed. The way they all sniffed from time to time. Perhaps the habit came from Grandad or even farther back. Then Rachel felt Rose's small hand tuck in under her arm and give a squeeze.

Rachel thought, it's been lovely driving into town.

They were passing the sliprail where her race against failing light began, satchel banging into her back.

CHAPTER FOURTEEN

House Full,
by Any Other Name

That's ruined it, Rachel thought, her head swimming from the effort of peering so hard. Look at them all. We're late. We'll never get in. We'd just have to be late, wouldn't we? One moment everything's perfect, the next it falls to pieces.

A family was crowded at the door to the porch arguing the right to enter.

They could hear a strident complaint as Dad turned the buggy in from the road and went past.

"Tell him I insist upon three seats together, the rest anywhere he likes. He can give me a measly three. It's Hamish being Hamish again. Boring little man. Let me talk to him."

It was a voice like the train whistle coming round through the gullies, except that the train was supposed to sound like a train and generally was a friendly creature.

"Did you hear her, Auntie Lizzie?"

"Everyone this side of the black stump heard her, as they usually do."

"If he can't give three to Mrs Fitz he can't give five to us, can he?"

"It all depends, child. It all depends."

"Are we late, Auntie Lizzie?" Rose cried.

"If we weren't it'd be a miracle. If your brilliant father had thought of telling me this morning that he might be taking us out this evening. . ."

"As you are well aware I was against it in principle this morning."

"Politics are no excuse."

Horses were tied to the rail, every rail, one beyond the other, blanketed, noses in feedbags, Dad in some astonishment driving past them a regrettable distance before he came to the end of the line, arriving there in the remote darkness behind the hall with the kind of sigh one kept for moments of the utmost cheerlessness.

"I'd never have credited it," he said. "It's like it was somewhere else. All these people turning up. I feel very bad. It makes me feel I've let you down. It'd have been better if I hadn't thought of it."

Rachel was developing a fit of the misery shakes. The exhaustion shakes. The pre-driving-home-in-bitter-disappointment shakes. Even going to bed had lost its appeal. When you travel such a long way to get somewhere, you want to get there. You don't want to find nothing when you arrive.

"I think you'd better make your way pretty quickly, Lizzie. I think I should've dropped you at the door."

"Why didn't you, then?"

"I didn't foresee this and you didn't foresee it either. So there's a good girl. We've all had a hard day. We all need a nice night out. See if they can squeeze us in."

"I'll good-girl you if they can't."

Poor Dad. No teasing left in him.

In sympathy, Rachel's spirits went sinking into the soupy dark round her feet and all she could do was try not to cry from disappointment and tiredness and from feeling for Dad.

"Aren't we going to get in?" Rose sniffled. "And my first time out at night that hasn't been to the church. Why'd all these people get here before us? Couldn't they have been later than us?"

Poor Rose.

"Not much use hurrying," Rennie said. "If it's full it's full. Like my workbook. I need tuppence on Monday for a new one."

Poor Rennie.

"Chah," said Rachel, though not out loud.

Poor Rachel.

Auntie Lizzie sighed, "Come along. We'll try. Bring your blankets. Bring yours, too, Frank, when you've fixed the ponies, if you can remember to bring yourself. Perhaps we can hang from the rafters like bats."

Poor Auntie Lizzie.

"We won't be needing blankets," Rennie said glumly, "except for keeping warm on the way back home. Which reminds me, I need a pencil."

"Nothing round here reminds me of a pencil," said Rose. "I hope we don't have to hang from the rafters like bats. I think that'd make me very tired. I might fall on my head."

"The supper plate, Rachel. Careful with it. I want the cream in the butterfly cakes looking pretty, not on the napkin looking squashed. Do you think you're awake enough to carry it? Do you think you can manage without walking into something?"

They hadn't been butterfly cakes at all an hour ago. Just common old fairy cakes in the cake tin then. Now they were split, with wings, and filled with clotted cream and dusted with icing sugar, looking as if they were fresh from the oven.

Grumble, grumble, thought Rachel. Once in a blue moon we get a night out and everyone in town gets there before us.

Like the toffee apples when they go sticky in Herberts' shop in sultry weather. Lucky if anyone from the gully gets one in a lifetime.

Living out there's like living in the next State. No one cares whether you're alive or dead. All thinking of themselves. All going out at night and getting there early. Not giving anyone else a chance to get in the door. Crowding the place out. Why couldn't they have stayed home and played tiddlywinks? Didn't any of them give a thought to getting home again in the cold afterwards? Brainless lot of people. Serve them right if they freeze.

All the family, except Dad, bustling back towards the hall.

Everyone anxious, picking their way round wheel ruts and random ridges of quartz and a few persistent puddles left lying from last Wednesday's rain, Rose almost running to keep up, Rennie making puffing sounds, Auntie Lizzie out in front holding up the hemline sweep of her green velvet, Rachel thinking, I did want to know about writing down my tunes. . . I did want to hear about being a famous organ player, everyone leaping to their feet and cheering. . . I did want to get a hand on a few cakes at supper time. . . It really would've been better if Dad hadn't thought of it, then I could've gone to bed. Then I'd have been sound asleep. Then I wouldn't have cared.

"All these people," Rose panted, "they must've come in from everywhere there is. I thought our dad was teasing about all the people when we came round the corner. He must be able to tell the future, too."

"If he could tell the future," Rennie said, "we'd have stayed home and he'd have been the famous one instead of Mrs Tombstone."

"Not Mrs Tombstone," said Rachel, "Mrs Headstone."

"Not Mrs Headstone," said Auntie Lizzie, "Mrs Headstrong. Not that it'll matter one way or the other if we don't get in."

"Will we have to go home?" Rose cried.

"Can't we look through the window," Rennie asked, "and save our money for treacle sticks on Monday?"

"That'd be all right for you, you great long stringy bean. The bottom of the window's higher than the top of my head and I've got to keep jumping to see in."

"How would you have made that interesting discovery, Rose Lefevre?" said Auntie Lizzie.

"I'm a bright little button, my teacher says."

"I've never heard her say it," said Rennie. "All I've

heard her say is, '*Rose, you've swallowed the cuckoo clock again'*."

"I go round finding out things," said Rose. "How many eggs in a magpie's nest. How many pipes in the drain under the road. How many books on Mr Hooke's library shelf. What would he want to read love stories for?"

"You talk too much," said Rennie, but Auntie Lizzie was in conversation with Mr Hamish Herbert, Secretary/Treasurer of the Hall Committee, presently rugged up from head to toe, seated upon a bentwood chair at a small oak table and presiding over the wide-open entry porch with a kind of frozen smugness or a chilled satisfaction, particularly when regarding the large tin of money received in aid of the Hall Committee and the stub ends of the innumerable tickets sold.

There really isn't room for us, Rachel moaned inside. Just look at him. Like the cat that got the cream.

"Well, well, well," Hamish Herbert was saying, "look what the earthworms have turned up. Troglodytes from the gully depths and about to plunge straight back again unrequited."

Horrible man he is, Rachel moaned inside. What's unrequited mean? I bet it means we don't get in. Bother, I say. I wish I could say it out loud. Bother all the way to Ballarat and bother all the way back again. I wish I could stamp my foot, the left one, because the right's got a sore toe.

"Five," Auntie Lizzie appeared to be saying, as if confidently expecting a favourable response, despite the strong feeling that a large proportion of the population of the district was already crowded inside. "Two adults and three children, thanking you, Mr Herbert, and I hope I don't have to repeat myself."

"Come, come, ma'amzelle. That's an attitude we can't justify in light of the fact that hope's dead round here for gentlefolk of the likes of vous and moi. I'll be pressing my own ear to the wall to catch a snatch of proceedings or hear nothing at all. Blame the Fitzes who went on in before you, creating their usual disturbance. Plus the assortment past counting of Hobsons, Crawfords and lesser branches of the Herbert family that preceded them. To say nothing of the O'Reillys and the O'Malleys from Gipsy Valley and the Dribbles from Ryan's and the multitude of Browns from Wensleydale, together with their cousins visiting from Creswick. We've got arms and legs poking out through the cracks in the walls in there if you care to take a look. A slight shift in the earth's crust would provoke some swift and painful amputations."

Silly man, thought Rachel. I suppose he thinks he's funny. Mr Hothead's right about something. And our Rose was right, too. They're here from everywhere. Taking our seats. Filling our hall, when they should've been at Creswick minding their own business.

"Two adults and three children, thanking you, Mr Herbert," said Auntie Lizzie very firmly.

"Haven't seen the like of it," said Hamish, "since Fannie Farmer came out with her recipes. Real drawcards, these famous Americans, ma'amzelle. Not the real Fannie Farmer either, I heard tell later. Some actress playing the part and most uncommon shapely, I recall, which was a compensation considering the subject. I well remember the bit where she forgot her lines and had to look them up in a cookery book. But this lady's the genuine article. I wouldn't be wanting any young actress feeling my bumps, not at my time of life, causing a disturbance I could do without. Not that that'll be provoking the Lefevres to any embarrassment, ma'amzelle. What you won't be seeing, you won't be getting upset about."

He's a dreadful man, thought Rachel. His wife and kids must have a terrible time. He's as bad as our father. Or worse. He's teasing us. At a time like this. When we're all miserable and anxious and still on the outside while everybody else is inside, including the Fitzes. They must be like it all their lives. Tease, tease, tease. From the time they're little boys. Always thinking they're so clever. I'm not in any hurry to get married. No fear. I think I'll wait for some fellow who doesn't know what tease means.

"I believe you heard me, Mr Herbert," Auntie Lizzie said. "Two adults and three children, if you don't mind."

"And I believe you heard me, ma'amzelle. Not a seat in the house as you'll observe for yourself if you poke your head round the door."

"Two adults. Three children. One quite small. She can sit in a lap."

"I'm so pleased I'm small," Rose said. "It's lovely being little. I'll get in and the rest of you won't."

"That's not nice of you, Rose," said Rennie, "since you're not much littler than me."

I'll shoot myself if I don't get in, Rachel thought, seeing I stopped being little years ago, but I'll shoot Mr Herbert first and do everyone a favour. Just as well the gun's in the front room and not in the buggy.

"You're not listening, ma'amzelle," Hamish said. "House full by five past eight. If you come staggering in at eight-twenty you'll not be getting farther unless you occupy the place by force. Taking your cue from Mrs Fitz, though she's better equipped for going backwards than anyone I presently see here, squeezing your rear end in and squeezing someone else's out."

"Mr Herbert!"

"Without starting a fight, ma'amzelle, or bringing the issue to the attention of the committee, in which event I'll be compelled to escort you to the street."

"You'll be compelled to do no such thing, Mr Herbert, under any circumstances of any kind whatsoever, and you'd forever regret it if you tried."

And another left eyebrow bit the dust, thought Rachel.

"No chairs, window sills, or the centre aisle to be occupied by children, ma'amzelle. That's the ruling of the committee. Don't blame me. I'm only the workhorse. All children to remain peaceful, refraining from pinchings, pokings, and punchings. We've got enough blackened eyes, blooded noses and bruised lips in there already. The place looks like something you ought to hose out. All children under the age of sixteen years to be seated firmly on the floor up the front in fixed positions. Girls to the left of the aisle, boys to the right, with a clear walking space up the middle to the foot of the stage, no movement of the sexes being permitted from one side to the other for juvenile communications when the lights go out. An express prohibiton to be borne in mind by young Juliet here whose presence confirms not only her fleetness of foot, but her attraction to the numerous young swains who were observed in hot pursuit this very evening through sections of the town and the paddocks beyond. Irrespective of age, good behaviour within these premises being obligatory or paddywhack the drumstick. Administered by me, personally. Out on their bouncing little bottoms. Down the steps. Bounce. Bounce. Bounce."

He's revolting, thought Rachel. Calling me Juliet! Who saw me running through the paddocks anyway? Where'd he get that from? If he knows, everybody knows. If everybody knows, where were they when I needed some help?

Auntie Lizzie said, "All my nieces behave, Mr Herbert, and you've said enough. Quite, quite enough."

"All children behave, ma'amzelle, some worse than others and others most appalling. Hoh there, and good evening to you, Monsieur Frank Lefevre! Wipe your feet please. You've been paddling through the horse muck again. And where'd you get the rose for the buttonhole at this time of year? Clever bit of waxwork there by the nimble-fingered ma'amzelle? Reckoning, no doubt, upon displacing Councillor Hobson tomorrow and occupying the presidential chair in a year or two? Hope springs eternal, they say, especially in the breast of a cultured man with an eighth-grade private education, reckoning on bringing a bit of new blood to the civic scene. And what's old Dave but the gravedigger voting himself the contracts in council, as everybody knows, though being a kind of composite Hobson, Herbert and Crawford, he's got seven votes out of ten to start with, blood being thicker than water, they say, as no doubt you confirmed this evening when dragging the body of that old drunk out of the dam at the mine. Bit of bad luck, monsieur, having to bury him tomorrow, not that he wouldn't have kept until next week. Being so nicely pickled. Going to cramp your style somewhat at the polling booth, not that your style can stand much cramping, though old Dave having got himself the contract'll have to be digging the hole, which'll be some small comfort for you in the short term, though not much consolation when the votes come to be counted. Got those feet clean, monsieur? Give them an extra wipe if you don't mind. No fun being a committee man, you know. After everyone's gone home to bed, there you are with the broom.

"I'll have two shillings and sevenpence ha'penny from you, ma'amzelle, seeing you're wisely holding the purse strings but preventing the movement of fresh air by blocking the gangway, *on* the understanding that you step smartly inside, keeping clear of the magic lantern and avoiding fist fights and the use of bad language, and taking the supper plate straight across to the kitchen out of harm's way, meaning that there supper plate is removed forthwith from the custody of young Juliet into adult protection... Well, well, well, look who's here now. Do I see more troglodytes rearing their curious heads from the depths of the gully, straining the laws of probability and exceeding our wildest expectations...?"

Oh glory, Rachel moaned inside. It gets worse and worse. Look at all those Crawford faces coming up the steps. *Our* Crawfords. Chrissie. Eddie, too, I'll bet. They must've been coming along behind. Chrissie said she wasn't coming at all! Why aren't I home in bed sound asleep?

"Too late, Mrs Crawford," Hamish was saying. "No

hope under Heaven for gentlefolk of the likes of you and
me. Stuffed to the eyebrows in there as you must surely
hear and see. Blame the Lefevres who go on in before you,
creating their usual disturbance. Barely the air to
breathe. Thick with Herberts, Hobsons, O'Reillys,
O'Malleys, Dribbles and Browns, and with all due respect
a few dozen Crawfords, both liquid and solid, poured in
around. To say nothing of assorted bits and pieces like
Fitzes, Baxters, Floods and Scrivens. It'll be known as
Black Friday in future years. The entire population of the
district suffocated in a single night. . ."

Crawfords were pressing ₂into the porch, Chrissie
obviously so full of news she was almost set to burst.

Into the hall went Rachel, carried on the surge of the
family, out of sight of Chrissie, out of sight of the
Crawfords, out of the reach of the voice of the awful
Hamish Herbert: "And what's this about our young Eddie
that's got the town buzzing? Generalissimo in the high
street and Romeo after hours? Wherefore art thou,
Romeo, Romeo. . ."

I can't bear it, Rachel thought. I'll die.

Inside she went, into the full house.

CHAPTER FIFTEEN

Every Man for Himself

"Every man for himself, I fear," Dad said.

Then no more Dad.

No Dad to lean on.

No Dad there.

How could Rachel have heard right? That phrase came from the sea. That phrase said the ship was going down. That phrase said do your own swimming or drown.

One moment all the other members of the family were making sounds of general satisfaction because they were inside the hall, not stranded on the rocks in the high street; the next there was a sole survivor, Rachel, left standing in a fog of faces and fans, with nowhere to sit and nowhere to go.

Everybody else in the lifeboat already gone.

Rachel marooned as usual on the ship fast going down.

A haze of motion. A confusion. Mainly the blessed fans. Fans made out of hats and newspapers and pocket wallets and handkerchiefs, even out of hands.

Fans flapping back and forth at the fevered air; the men at it as well, swishing at the air.

And faces.

My goodness. Faces like a dream you'd be wanting to wake up from. Faces flushed from the generated heat of the wagon-loads of human flesh arrayed around, and from the radiated heat of kerosene gas lamps hanging from the rafters, and from the pressure of being crushed in like an overpacked flower bed at the end of a torrid day. All the flowers trying to hold themselves up, but wilting. All the flowers hoping to smell like violets, but smelling more like decomposing cabbages.

That horrible Hamish Herbert's the lucky one, thought
Rachel. Out there in the porch. Out there in the cold. In
the lovely fresh air.

Not a window was open and there never would be,
short of a major explosion. Every window was stuck firm
with coats of paint in layers about five years apart and
up to forty years deep, every window streaked with con-
densation, all looking like frosted glass with rain falling
on them from the inside, as if defying the laws of Nature
and probability.

Air available for breathing was best not breathed at
all. That silly story about suffocation. That stupid man.
Did suffocation creep up on you unawares? Or did it hit
you suddenly on the head?

All the people, despite the good humour, were sniffing
and sneezing and coughing and sounded like Mr
Hothead's herd kept waiting past milking time, each
person dragging in any scrap of oxygen passing by with
the kind of greed or need that gave no thought to the
requirements of others, each giving up in exchange for
his or her modest measure of oxygen the total of his or her
germs in a continuing issue of noxious vapours escaping
round the sides of their handkerchiefs.

More germs, in Rachel's anxious estimate, than she'd
be finding outside between here and the next corner of
the road, counting in the pub, the stables, and the
drains.

Anyone going home with less than the plague would be
doing fine.

"Children up the front," people said to her.

Well, she knew that. She was taking her time. She'd
done enough running for one night.

"Move on down the front, lass," people said to her.
"You can't stand there, you know."

I'm not standing anywhere, she could have said and
very nearly did. Can't you see I'm moving?

"Bless me, dear," Miss Nora said to her, "what are you doing here? Shouldn't you be home in bed?"

You're the right one to ask that question, Rachel thought of saying back again, but didn't.

"Well, well," people said to her, "if it's not Rachel, the femme fatale."

I'm not a femme fatale. I'm alive and well. I can't help it if I look half dead. Consider yourselves lucky you don't look the same.

"Lift your boots," people said to her. "Don't trip over us, girl, not with feet as big as those."

How could I trip over anyone here? I couldn't step high enough. And I might have a big toe half as long as the rest of me, but I have a very dainty foot that I much admire when I'm sitting in the bath.

"Are you all right, young lady?" Carter Hooke said to her.

She nodded.

"We'll need to make sure it never happens again, young lady."

She nodded.

Then it dropped upon her like a blanket!

Her hands were empty!

The butterfly cakes!

Not a crumb to be seen.

Not a chipped edge of the plate.

What have I done with them? Oh misery, misery. Some rotten thief has stolen my cakes.

"Hey, you, Rachel, you can't stand here."

I don't know why everything's so complicated. Why are things always so difficult for me? Other people just walk in and sit down.

"Hey, you, Rachel Lefevre. We don't want you here. You'll give the place a bad name. Boys on this side. Girls over there. Specially you."

Do you think for one moment, Rachel thought, that I'd

be sitting anywhere near you, Rodney Herbert. I'm real
glad to see you've got a black eye. I hope it hurts. I hope it
closes up so you can't see out of it. I hope you walk into a
door and blacken the other one.

"Do you propose to stand there all night, girl? Why
don't you sit down?"

Well, sir, as soon as I find somewhere to sit, that's what
I'll be doing. I'm as anxious about it as you are. But as
you can see, if you're fair, you've got to agree...

"Gor blimey, Rachel, not there! You can't sit there.
Stick a pin in her, will you!"

It was a real rough sea that had blown up, every wave a
line of packed seats, or a line of flushed faces, or a line of
fans, or a line of big mouths all flapping to and fro. Come
here. Go there. Not here. Not there. Sit down. Stand up.
My goodness, girl, do you think you're made of glass like
a windowpane?

It was easy for them. You could be real clever when you
were sitting down. When you weren't in danger of being
thrown out. Down the steps. Bounce. Bounce. Bounce.

"Up you get, girl. That will not do! You're blocking the
aisle again. If you can't squeeze in somewhere, out of
sight, out of everyone's way, you'll have to go home.
When the sardine tin's full, it's full."

"Yes, sir," Rachel said. "I understand. I'm doing my
best, sir."

"Over here, Rachel. Hurry yourself."

No one else had a voice like that. It had to be Rennie.
But where?

"Over here!"

Over where?

Rennie and Rose, the disappearing sisters. Dad, the
disappearing father. Auntie Lizzie, the disappearing
aunt. It was terrible being the eldest kid and forever
being pushed from pillar to post. It was beneath the
dignity of one's position. In Chrissie's house Chrissie was
the *youngest*, yet she bossed them all. Except her dad.

And bossed him half the time.

There was Rachel's dad, a bit like a squashed tomato, standing against the rear wall with Mr Hothead, both of them with their mouths open like everybody else, but Rachel couldn't hear. Probably saying to each other: "What's all this about my daughter and your son?" — or — "What's all this about my son and your daughter?" — or directly across the crowded room to Rachel — "Come here, go there, not here, not there, sit down, stand up, go home you wicked girl and run all the way on your own."

I can't bear it, thought Rachel. I'll die.

A hand closed on her arm as if the dreaded moment had arrived; horrible Hamish Herbert about to bounce her down the steps and out into the street; Rachel making a strangled sound, her heart going thump, no head getting read, no Mrs Headstone from Sacrasomewhere; but the face that came round the side was *Chrissie's*.

Oh, lovely Chrissie. I'm so glad you're Chrissie and not that horrible Mr Hamish. You're the lifeboat coming back to the sinking ship.

I'm saved. It's my friend.

With Chrissie you're never left standing. With Chrissie you're never last in the queue. With Chrissie you'd never die in a famine. Rachel would though, if Chrissie wasn't there.

"Eddie," said Chrissie against her ear, with intensity, with excitement, with the promise of incredible revelations to come, "has been caught red-handed. Has he ever! As if you didn't know."

"Not here," Rachel said wildly. "Please, please, Chrissie. I couldn't bear it."

"We're all here, you know," Chrissie hissed, "not Eddie though. Not on your life. Not that Eddie. He's sent to bed. I bet he's lying on his top side though, not on his bottom side. Dad; I thought he'd break his hand. History repeats itself, you know. Maybe like Grandad's hand. What Dad broke of Eddie's, though, Heaven knows."

There were times when Chrissie was a trial.

"Will you sit down there, you two girls blocking the aisle. It's due to start any time now."

"We're *about* to sit down, Mr Brown," Chrissie said, "we're just summoning up the strength."

"You won't be sitting here, Chrissie Crawford. There's no room here. You go and paint the fence."

"The very row for us, I think," Chrissie said, "among all these nice friendly loving cousins. Don't take any notice of them, Rachel. You're the church organist. Make 'em move. Go on, shove up in there. Make room for the church organist or God'll strike you dumb."

"I've lost my butterfly cakes," Rachel said miserably. "I don't know why everything happens to me. I held on tight all the time. I was so careful. Auntie Lizzie'll be so mad."

"Don't know why she should be. She took them off to the kitchen."

"She didn't," Rachel said.

"Are you asleep or something? Are you still out there in the dark?"

"I don't know," Rachel said.

"What are those scratches on your face?"

"How would I know? I can't see them."

"Are you girls going to sit down or am I going to call Mr Herbert to throw you out?"

Chrissie said, "I bet you do know what those scratches are. I bet I know, too. Do I ever. You getting chased over fences and all. *Go on, you lot in there, shove up. Make room. Push, push.*"

They moved. The whole row of them. All the ones that were cousins and the few that weren't, and the character up at the far end jammed in against the wall started looking highly feverish, hair disordered, tongue hanging out, trying to make breathing room, but Chrissie was folding up her blanket, making a cushion of it, then sitting on the floor. "You, too," she said to Rachel.

Rachel folded her blanket in much the same manner,

made a cushion and a narrow place for herself next to the aisle, but Mary Foley was standing there.

Honest, if it wasn't one thing it was another.

It must have been Mary's call she'd heard coming along the road. Oh dear. Oh dear.

The toes of Mary's scuffed and muddy boots were almost touching Rachel's knee.

The *simplest* things turned into the most *complicated* decisions of what was right and what was wrong. They really did.

Rachel tried not to notice. Well, even Mary's best clothes smelt of mice. It was extra hard at school, specially by the end of the week.

Mary sat at Rachel's desk because no one else would share.

"Move up, please," Mary said. "It's me, Rachel, your friend. Let me in or I'll have to go home and I won't see the lovely lady."

"Off you trot then," said Chrissie. "No room here. Only Methodists here."

Other kids piped up, "Off you trot, Mary Foley."

Rachel's eyes had to go up to her. It wasn't right, trying to make out she wasn't there. Mary was the cross that Rachel had to bear. Sometimes the thought occurred to her that God had let her play the organ for nearly four whole years because she was nice to Mary.

Rachel said, "Move up, Chrissie. We can make a little bit more. Push. Please, Chrissie."

Chrissie almost shrieked into her ear. "You can't mean it!"

Suddenly, Rachel *did* mean it. You couldn't be the doormat all your life. She looked Chrissie in the eye. She glared. She bared her teeth. "You're my friend. Do as I say."

Chrissie recoiled and couldn't even mumble, just shoved, and the character away up at the far end pinned against the wall wailed a bitter protest, "Fair go. I'm go-

ing to be as skinny as a leaf and as tall as a tree. Me mum
won't know me."

Mary Foley sat on the floor, no blanket for a cushion,
so Rachel halved the thickness of her own and doubled
the width of it.

"Thank you," Mary said. "I knew you would. Did they
catch you?"

Inside Rachel wanted to fade away, but managed to
say, "No. No."

"What about Eddie though?"

"I don't know anything about Eddie."

Rachel could feel Dad's eyes boring in on the back of
her head. Oh by golly.

Go away, Dad. Leave me be. Have you really got to
talk to Mr Hothead? Have you really got to believe
everything you hear?

On the left side Chrissie whispered strongly against
Rachel's ear, "What'd you let her in for?"

Out of the side of her mouth Rachel said, "You know
why."

Into Rachel's ear Chrissie said, "I can smell her from
here."

Into Chrissie's ear Rachel said, "Perhaps she can smell
you, too."

"Oh, thank you," said Chrissie. "That's real friendly.
Thank you very much."

So Rachel directed her attention to the stage, suffering
the shivers and shakes inside, taking note of everything up
there as if the observation were a matter of high importance. A table to one side, three bentwood chairs, and a
double white bedsheet hanging in the centre of the wall,
starched as stiff as a shirt collar. A stupefying achieve-
ment.

Chrissie was busy again at Rachel's left ear.

"My brother, you know. He's really done it. We had my
Uncle Jack at our door. The boys frightening you. He'd
heard. Eddie chasing you. He'd heard. Guess who told?

Cousin Tim. He was with Eddie, chasing too."

Rachel hissed back, "If your Uncle Jack knew what was going on, why didn't he come and help me?"

"You were home with your Auntie Lizzie before Tim told. But Eddie told more."

"Eddie told?"

"Eddie owned up to it all."

She couldn't believe. There was nothing she could say.

"Everyone knows. Even about your satchel down the hole. Eddie's too! Eddie lost his and didn't know. Gregor's going fishing for them tomorrow with his rod and line."

Mary Foley making whispering noises near her right ear, Chrissie Crawford making whispering noises into her left. Like being a rug getting beaten from both sides. Everybody knowing everything except her. Even knowing more.

The smell of mice to the right, and to the left the smell of something potent that might have been sold at Miss Harriet Hobson's Haberdashery Shoppe as cologne suitable for young girls. Probably sold last Christmas to Gregor or Angus or Dougal or James or some other burly Crawford brother.

Chrissie nudging with her elbow into Rachel's ribs, Rachel's ribs being so near the surface she had to hiss back, "You're hurting me. You're making me sore." She almost said it so Chrissie could hear.

Chrissie, meanwhile, went on whispering loud and clear, "Dad. He was jumping. He was boiling. He was screaming, 'You've had your time. You're finished. No Continuation School for you. You larrikin. You lout. Terrorising everybody in town. Half-killing that poor girl of fright. You can chop wood for a living like the rest of the witless wonders.'"

"That's not fair," Rachel whispered back. "That's cruel. He didn't do any harm except to Willie's nose and who cares tuppence for that!"

"Dad was screaming. Screaming at Eddie, 'You know I

can't stand being under the same roof as Hamish Herbert who's the biggest pain I know. But you're the new champ. You beat him hollow. No one in this house wants to be under the same roof as you. We're leaving you to it, Edward Charles Crawford, you blot on the family name, and that's saying something with all the deadhead Crawfords we've got living round here.'"

"It's not fair," Rachel sighed. "He didn't do any harm."

"Eddie, he was jumping, dodging that hand, Dad whacking into chairs and walls, Dad screaming, 'Stand still so I can hit you, you horrible kid, you slimy pale pink worm.' Eddie, he was screaming too. 'Let me walk her home nice and proper then. Let me wait in town Tuesdays and Fridays till she's finished her lesson. She's not safe on her own having to put up with horrible kids like me.'"

"That's all right," Rachel said wearily, so wearily, as if she'd just crossed a high hill and at last could sit down.

"What's all right?" whispered Chrissie hoarsely.

"I'm not scared of Eddie. I'll ask my dad to agree."

The door at the back of the stage swung open and Councillor Dave Hobson appeared in full magnitude, coming on in, whilst behind him the door closed as if by some remote and marvellous mechanism, probably the hand of one of his many sons.

Every kid in the place, even Chrissie with her mouth wide open, immediately shut up, it being generally known from past events that Dave would be knocking senseless, brainless and boneless any kid who talked out of turn or misbehaved; Rachel at once thinking, fancy getting saved by the big ape, but noting, even in her moment of gratitude, the huge orange-coloured badge upon his lapel.

That unscrupulous old villain.

On top of all the dreadful things he'd been saying about Dad for the past month, here was his final, ultimate, *unscrupulosity*. A badge, as big as a bread and butter plate, *Vote for Dave*, with red, white and blue ribbons hanging from it as if he were the King's special representative.

Dad wasn't wearing a badge. Dad didn't own one. Dad didn't even have a chair to sit on. He had to lean against the wall, all squashed up, where no one would even see him or know that he was there.

"Good evenin', ladies and gentlemen," Dave boomed from the edge of the stage, offering no such welcome to the boys and girls, offering them instead a threatening downward glare and towering over them from the very edge as if giving some consideration to the idea of falling on top of them and crushing out a few lives.

Rachel was incensed.

"The time o' day," boomed Dave, raising his eyes to his adult constituents, "bein' eighty-thirty precisely, let's have some hush." Which silenced the grown-ups also, for not only could Dave fill a grave with his shoulders during the course of his periodic digs, his voice could stop a runaway horse.

Keeping dead quiet and out of reach of him and looking like an angel on a short visit from Heaven was self-preservation if you were a kid, though what you had to say about it behind his back was another matter. What the grown-ups had to say wasn't much different, except that on election days they voted him back in.

Dave, meanwhile, was fixing his adult constituents with a faintly sinister grin that said, "Vote for me tomorrow, as usual, and I won't be needin' to beat your brains out. But give your vote to Lefevre and Heaven save us from ruin. Give a thought to the Sun Never Sets Mining Company that went bust down on Yellow Plains, and to the Southern Comfort that went bust out at Ryan's, and to the Golden Bracelet that went bust at Arrowhead. One thing in common. Desperate days begin when Frank Lefevre walks in. I wouldn't have him near any mine o' mine. Nor near any Council either."

"Your Hall Committee," boomed Dave, "works year in and year out under my tireless direction, searchin' the world for the very best entertainment and instruction to divert you at prices you can afford. The latter bein' a severely limitin' factor that has in no way applied tonight. As your longstandin' chairman during me four terms as shire councillor, about to begin me fifth, there's never been an occasion that's pleased me more than seein' you here tonight from far and wide, some faces but rarely on the scene in many a year, all catching the enthusiasm that has swept the district, for tonight we have a real catch. . .

"Ladies and gentlemen, during her grand tour of the South Seas this gracious lady has generously come to this small place, this husk of former glories I might call it, entirely donatin' her services to help your committee to keep this building in good nick, so that we have a place for sharing our happy times with each other. It's with pride that I present her to you, one of the most famous readers of heads in all the world, Mrs Ernest Headstrong of Sacramento, USA."

He'd done it again. Won his election. Hardly needing Dad's help at all.

The stage door opened and in she came, aged, gentle, in a green velvet gown, bringing some of the secrets and excitements of the future with her, and Rachel knew, just knew, that the lovely lady would be calling her up to the stage and placing her hands upon her head, as long as she could remain awake after the lights went out.

Afterword

Rachel Elizabeth (Bess), eldest daughter of Franci John
(Frank) and Elizabeth Arabella (Bell), was borr near
Melbourne, Australia, on 11 June 1892, and shortly afterwards went to live on the goldfields where her fathe had
grown up. Her family, coming from the Channel Islands,
was of French origin. (Lefevre, however, is a fictitious
name.) Her younger sisters were Elsie Wren and Muriel
Rose — Elsie and Mu!

In Melbourne, in 1918, Rachel Elizabeth married
Francis Gordon (Frank), one-time Presbyterian home
missionary, whose family came from the English
midlands. He had a droll sense of humour and of course
turned out to be a terrible tease. Some things, it seems,
were never meant to be. He died too soon, in 1935, aged
forty-seven.

The two sons of Rachel Elizabeth and Francis Gordon
are known by their given names. The younger sings. The
elder writes. Both inherited the compulsion to tease, thus
regularly placing themselves in positions of censure they
rarely deserve.

Referred to, but not appearing in this story which is
fiction based upon possibilities and probabilities and real
people and actual events, is Susan Jane, Auntie Susie, the
much loved great-aunt of my own boyhood. Aunt Clara,
in *Josh*, grew out of her.

Rachel Elizabeth, in her ninety-fourth year as I finish
this book, is now blind, but when she comes to tea she is
still able to play from memory almost any hymn you care
to name.

This book is dedicated to her with love.

147

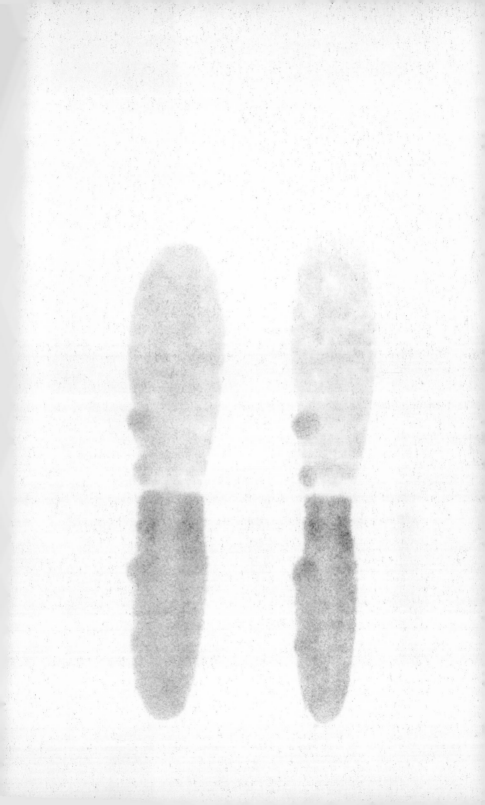